Finely tuned to dialogue and shifting
Harris' fast-moving prose is as pris
world she evokes. Her *Canterbury T*
rich with migrant collisions and collusions.

John Agard
Playwright, poet and children's writer

Six hundred years on, here are Canterbury's new pilgrims, as diverse and garrulous as Chaucer's were, and speaking in a variety of Englishness which, like Chaucer's, are hybrid and poetic. Maggie Harris creates stories about the nitty-gritty of 'ordinary' folk's lives, which, although often dealing with tragedy, pettiness, and awareness of loss, are also infused with warmth, humour and optimism. Each brief story or sketch gives voice to a character – a taxi driver, a young student, a politician's wife, a mother, a Chinese restaurant owner and a lover of Country and Western music – whose tales quickly draw you in, and sometimes, unwittingly, suggest a world of experience.

Lyn Innes
Emeritus Professor of Postcolonial Literatures,
University of Kent

In this book, Maggie Harris takes us by the hand and says, look again. Look, and listen to the people who matter, these everyday people we might otherwise miss whether we are on the train, in a Chinese take-away, sitting next to an empty bar-stool. This is vivid and compelling writing, but most of all – like the original – it's great storytelling.

Sarah Salway
Canterbury Laureate

Maggie Harris has published five collections of poetry; her first, *Limbolands* (1999), won the Guyana Prize for Literature 2000. Her memoir of growing up in Guyana, *Kiskadee Girl,* was published by Kingston University Press in 2011. She has also recorded a CD of poems for children, *Anansi Meets Miss Muffet.*

A writer and an artist, she has been International Teaching Fellow at Southampton University, a literature festival organiser and runs workshops for both children and adults. Her exhibition, From Broadstairs with Love, ran at The Old Lookout Gallery, Broadstairs, in June 2012.

www.maggieharris.co.uk

This work acknowledges the support of New Writing South.

CANTERBURY TALES ON A COCKCROW MORNING

Also by Maggie Harris

Selected Poems, Guyana Classics Library (2011)
Kiskadee Girl (2011)
After a Visit to a Botanical Garden (2010)
From Berbice to Broadstairs (2006)
Limbolands (1999)

Co-edited with Ian Dieffenthaller
Sixty Poems for Haiti (2010)

Canterbury Tales on a Cockcrow Morning

Maggie Harris

Cultured Llama Publishing

First published in 2012 by
Cultured Llama Publishing
11 London Road
Teynham, Sittingbourne
ME9 9QW
www.culturedllama.co.uk

ISBN 978-0-9568921-6-4

Printed in Great Britain by Lightning Source UK Ltd

Cover design based on an original by Mark Holihan, adapted
and amended by Bob Carling

Contents

Preface

These short stories were inspired by an earlier writing of the title story, *A Canterbury Tale on a Cockcrow Morning,* itself inspired by a number of linked events and evolutions. Whilst at Kent University during the 1990s I went along to several World Music events comprising music, dance and drumming in Canterbury and at WOMAD.

My degree in African Caribbean Studies at an English university opened my eyes and sustained and developed my sense of self as a migrant living in Kent. British travellers to other parts of the world imported ideas they had encountered whilst abroad; Peruvian panpipes played outside the Cathedral wall. Historically and through landmarks, Chaucer's Canterbury was very much in evidence, but the celebration of diverse cultures through their appropriation in local festivals led me to think about the new people who were either transient or settling in Canterbury.

What were these new migrants bringing to Canterbury? How would the city welcome or change them? Physical changes in the development of Canterbury such as the new shopping precinct were also ongoing. As a regular visitor, student and working artist in Canterbury, I have witnessed and been part of the evolution of the city from 1972 onwards.

The title story was initially published by Urban Fox Press and went through many transformations. But the bones of the story remain: languages butt up against each other: Standard English, Creole, Spanish, the language of writing itself, and an imagined Chaucerian, poetic voice of the city, who makes the link between past and present.

As a poet, I am always inspired by the spoken word, and I have borrowed some elements of the storyteller's form. Naturally this collection is by nature, limited in form, determined by space. A million other tales and other perspectives exist, mine is a small effort to make note and celebrate new additions to this rich and rewarding city, which not only educated me, but integrated me.

My thanks go out to New Writing South who believed these tales were worth writing.

Maggie Harris

Prologue:
The Journey into Canterbury

Welcome

The first thing we must not presume is that we are coming from London. Oh, they might have done that in Chaucer's day, it being the centre and all that. But things have changed. There are, as they used to say about Rome, many roads that lead, so we'll just substitute train tracks for 'roads'. If anything it's good advertising for Railtrack (nearly said British Rail then; that dates me.)

I can tell you a thing or two about trains – you remember the ones with the sealed carriages with their own compartments you dared anyone else to enter? The sliding windows and the corridors where you loitered, had a fag, tempted fate by leaning your head out the windows? Ah, those were almost like the steam trains we gloried in as children, whistling their way through banana plantations and shuddering to a stop through lazy dogs and the white gleam of the city. But that first Kent train – my younger sister peering closely at something we would learn was called graffiti – turning to me and in a loud voice and saying 'What does W A N K mean?' O what babes we were!

I wouldn't think many of you would come on foot, bus perhaps, bicycle maybe, horse not a chance! Unless you come by sea to Whitstable (in which case you'll still have to take a bus, or taxi if you're minted! – into Canterbury), points of departure may be Ramsgate, Folkestone or the Highspeed. It might have been interesting to gather a tale from Manston Airport but not many fly in there now, not unless you count a hand of bananas. From Ramsgate now, where I think they've re-instated the ferry to Dunkerque (I can't keep up with it all, open the route, close the route blah blah blah), Canterbury is a mere twenty minutes on the train. With any luck you might be witness to some interesting shenanigans like the unfortunate Afghan who'd come this far without a ticket and the inspector wasn't having any of it. Treated the poor bloke that bad I tell you. Handed him over to the cops at Canterbury with such relish you could almost hear his hands washing themselves. I felt for the Afghan, I really did, wondering how far he'd come, how he crossed the channel, how many had ripped him off on the way and who he'd left behind.

You have a choice of stations in Canterbury, West or East; both land you slap bang in the city, West via Ashford (International now, be precise) and East, where your journey will be pastoral and green, stopping through such villages as Littlebourne; the only thing that spoils it will be the odd lout or verbally acute young woman all striving to make as much an impression on you as they do on each other. I bore witness to a little old lady, if you'll excuse the euphemism, taking on such a pair at Sandwich one day, telling them firmly and bravely to be quiet and have some regard for their fellow passengers. Believe it or not, after some raucous laughter in which one advised the other they were being told off, they did pack it in! I don't know whether our fellow passengers felt as ashamed as I did that some Miss Marple had done our job for us. But don't let me get started on that generation thing, I'll never shut up.

That line deposits you at Canterbury East, within sight of the famous old city wall, some of which I do believe we have the Romans to thank for. There's been a tradition of burning and pillaging in East Kent, if it wasn't Horsa it was Hengist or some-such. That's what makes me laugh, what a wonderful mongrel nation we are, to misquote the wonderful Nobel Poet Derek Walcott, with all that Roman and Viking and Huguenot input, what's a few new migrations to worry about? As my dear old gran used to say, you can't have soup without pepper and salt.

From Blighty now, me old dears (and that *is* how they used to talk still, back in the seventies), I can name you every stop through to Canterbury. Stopped off at every one of them too, for this reason or that, some more important than others… Good way to know the country when you don't drive. It was through all these little journeyings that these stories came. Chilham I recall especially fondly; a lovely elderly lady who had befriended my mother had the archetypal cottage, and there we had tea and I stuck a nappy pin right through my new baby's skin. Don't worry, she lived to tell the tale. Ah those were the days when they had jousting at Chilham Castle too … how much more English can you get? But alas – it was sold off and the jousting stopped pronto. And later still, when I went through my feminist period, I walked, I truly did, with hardened women in boots from Wye to Chilham through fields of rape and gullies of nettles. Toughened me, that did.

Yes, I've certainly been there and done that, seeing this little part of Kent through alien eyes everything is always new, although influenced by Constable's paintings, and oast houses. Yes! I can tell you a tale about an oast house too! That's where the baby learnt to walk, going round and round those circular walls on the inside with soft palms covered in chocolate which the snooty owner charged an extra tenner for. But I digress; due to my age I tend to wander, let's visit some of these characters I've met along the way. I may interrupt now and then, or just leave them to get on with it. I may even return at the end with a few words, if I haven't fallen asleep myself.

The Calypsonians of Ramsgate

Right, we're in the seventies, and there were these three guys. Three roaring rollicking, arrogant boys with manes of black Irish hair and hands as inconsistent as birds. Eyes rolled at the mention of their names. Teachers expelled them from school. Girls gladly raised their skirts in the back of borrowed Fiestas or behind the waltzers on the ramshackle seafront at night.

These were glory days, when dole cheques went straight in the Red Lion or the Royal Standard, when the promise of a painting and decorating job was mildly appealing, especially in the summer when bare chests on the tops of scaffolding was reality bill-boarding. The freedom of the town was theirs.

Jamie, Drake and Errol; their mother had had a penchant for Hollywood movies and stars, and had pinned her daydreams on her boys even as they continually failed to exhibit any of the romance. But there were plenty of derring-dos, and face it, was Mr Flynn a gentleman?

Seaside towns then were only just beginning to die. Some described them as fading, a sign of the times; who wanted waltzers and creaking Ferris wheels when foreign holidays beckoned? The Costas were cheap, as was Greece, and if you wanted black sand, Lanzarote. So the word on the street about poor old Ramsgate was that it was a *dive*, it was *ranking*. Who the fuck wanted to stay in a place where only the Channel prevented the frogs from finishing what they always wanted to do since fucking Henry's days man? But even as everyone dissed the place, apart from one or two who emigrated to Amsterdam or Wales, none of them would live anywhere else. If you wanted a slice of the good life there was Canterbury and London, there and back in a day. On the train of course, less you knew someone with a motor.

The words that fell off the boys' lips sloshed like the Guinness on the sodden bar towels. Their elbows grew white with ownership on the laminated rosewood, and their leather jackets settled securely on the bar stools they barely perched on, shifting only for the bravest or cutest bit of *stuff* – eyes lined with liquid liner, mouth pale with lip-gloss, hair like Farrah Fawcett's.

The old men raised their rheumy eyes through a haze of cigarette smoke from their dark corners by the door, obliged by the pint Jamie might buy them having just been paid for doing up that flat up Westcliff Road some London punter had bought. The old guys were a fountain of knowledge from Henry Tudor to Hitler, *been there mate, 1944.* And foreign invasions continued to happen each summer; flocks of Scandinavian blondes descending through the channels of the local language school, their tentative steps through the doors of The Standard bringing the conversation to a halt. The glint of Ramsgate sand on those golden arms sent hands reaching deep in pockets for a pound note for a half of shandy. Foreign chicks were the business, they all agreed; here for a few weeks then bingo, gone. Not like those local birds scrounging pints and fags off you all night then glued to your arm when they found out you had a lift to the Bali Hai in Margate. The next thing you know they thought you were fucking going out together! Enough of that shit. Those foreign blokes though, they were a right laugh; see their tight asses in white trousers racing off along the seafront on a Saturday night when your money ran out and you were looking for a laugh.

Friday nights were the business: pound notes fluttered between fingers, packets of Embassy and John Players passed over the bar. Shoulders relaxed and laughter cut across the jukebox playing Hendrix or Springsteen or that Commodores shit the chicks all loved.

But it didn't take much for the place to explode. Some *oik* spilling drink on a jacket, some wanker pushing in. Before you knew it fists were out there, knuckles curled round collars. Depending on how many pints had been consumed, that might be all. But if the mood spread, before you could say Red Rum any chairs or tables that weren't screwed down would be flying like missiles. The times windows were smashed were countless. On a Saturday morning the windows would be boarded up and you'd wander in to face a sullen landlord snapping *no way them bastards coming back in 'ere, fucking banned the lot of 'em*. But you'd catch sight of Jamie swigging a pint at The Royal and catch his eye and say *good last night then?* And he'd grin and say *Bloody right! Arseholes need teaching a lesson*. The ban might last a week or two, but business was business and after a mouthful of warnings the boys would be back there again, leaning their elbows on the bar.

Friday night was disco night; Margate loomed, the Bali Hai, the Gavroche, the Hippocampo. *Anyone going to*

Margate? Taxis were fascist, like Thatcher. Much more appropriate to scrounge a lift from the only one of two blokes who owned a motor. The dance floor was the chance the girls got to catch a guy, fuelled with lagers or Dubonnets, bodies clad in maxi-dresses or low-slung hipster trousers with halter-neck tops. That was the time too to see the divide between the girls who danced round their handbags and those who sat in the dark corners of the disco, heads low with the guys over packets of Rizla and lighters warming minuscule nuggets of hope.

And that's the path the boys went down. Not for them the fascist path of colleges and wanker bankers. This was the one life, see? Who wanted shit like houses and neat drives and two weeks in the Costas? People with jobs and cars were wankers. Life was your mates and beating the state at their game. Their voices, full of resolution, grievances and piss-takes, were left over from the revolution of cheese-cloth shirts, the workers revolution of Ramsgate. Mick Jagger was a ponce. Ask them round and they took the world to pieces, quoting Nostradamus (who they'd all read, though their former teachers at Holy Cross might have disbelieved this). They were like that Alf Garnett character off the telly. They threw aside fashion and *House Beautiful* magazines with scorn as they forked Vesta curries off their mates' girlfriends with relish.

The girls who loved them fought the good fight. They fell for their energetic beauty, their vociferousness, their disdain, the ripple and conviction of their arguments. They saw the good souls beneath their armadillo skin. Drake's girlfriend Caris in particular, risen to the right of that title by giving birth to little Drake, took his cavalier pretences with good grace. Agreed with everything he said and did, responded to his *Give us a fag, slag;* turned a blind eye to the nights he didn't come home. (After her mum threw her out Drake had had the grace to find her a flat even though he insisted he didn't live there.) She knew he loved her, his first jail sentence had come on her behalf after he'd thrown the man from the Housing Benefit down the flight of stairs.

It was Caris who was with Jamie that night he choked to death on a fishbone. They'd gone for an Indian after she and Drake had had a row over some girl in the pub and Jamie had taken her to cheer her up. For the life of her she didn't know why Jamie went for fucking fish. He always had chicken tikka. One minute he was cracking her up with some joke and the next he was coughing and clutching at his throat and going blue in the face. When she realised that he wasn't mucking about it was all panic stations, glasses of water from the flustered waiters, then the telephone call for the ambulance after Jamie's eyes rolled backwards and his head flopped forwards. And right to the end his prophecy about the Government came through: for only recently they'd shut down the A&E at Margate and the ambulance had had to scream all the way to Canterbury by which time Jamie was dead.

Drake and Errol went mental after that. Started hanging about with blokes from London and Brighton eager to find markets for the little innocuous envelopes that changed hands underneath the pub tables. Drake grew a beard and went about with a Trinidadian called Clyde whose right to be in the pubs and clubs and eventually on the housing estate he defended with his mouth and fists, and from whom he was initiated to the Calypso records of Mighty Spoiler, Sparrow, and Prince Buster. They ska-ed their way to Ramsgate's hot nightclub Nero's and Club Caprice in Margate, doing business to the blind eyes of the bouncers whilst rocking to *No Woman, No Cry*. Trainers and jeans from Ramsgate market became trainers and jeans from Burton's.

Caris had another baby, and on one of Drake's releases from Sheppey they got married at Ramsgate Registry Office followed by a buffet at the Standard.

After fighting off the attentions of girls called Tracy and Dawn, Errol had fallen for an Irish girl called Siobhan, a nurse at Ramsgate hospital he'd met one lunchtime in the Artillery Arms in between wallpapering a flat for a mate. Siobhan tried to lure him to the idea of the straight and narrow, but all he could get was a job at Tilmanstone Colliery (which, to be fair, he stuck for a week) but he got the shakes even thinking about it – *that fucking lift man, drops like a fucking stone pits of hell man* – and went back to the gratuitous and temporary nature of the work he most enjoyed. All in all, it was meant, he said, eye on the telly with the news of impending closures and miners meaner than him pointing their fingers at the TV cameras and spitting.

When Drake's coughing became noticeable, when he allowed himself to be dragged to the doctors by Caris whose resolute nature had evolved to a nervous laugh after years of being slapped about and shouted down, and on one occasion dragged by the hair down Ramsgate High Street, they were all in for a shock. Drake had cancer of the throat. The years of smoking did not go without comment. The thin warning line on the fag packet suddenly had some relevance. Nobody wanted to elaborate on other experimental ways of getting high, super large reefers, milk bottles, an authentic Moroccan pipe. Grass was the killer, they nodded to themselves, home-grown the worse, always burning the back of your throat.

Hope filled their spirits for a while. Drake went for the operation and even when they took his voice box out it didn't get him down, didn't stop him going down the pub for a pint which he poured down the tube in his throat; though more and more he went with Caris.

When he died it was like the tide had gone out and wasn't coming back. His bar stool stood vacant. Punters went about shaking their heads *you heard about Drake man?* The guy had been larger than life, nothing had fazed him, head to head with coppers the lot. If that could happen to him, it could happen to anyone; life was truly shit man. At least the glass-topped hearse gave him the dignity he deserved.

Siobhan goes to see Errol every day now. She takes the train to Canterbury from Ramsgate, gets a bus to the hospital, sits with him. She never knows what to take him. Grapes were out, as were drinks. He hasn't eaten or drunk for a year now, the tube in his stomach carries everything he needs. Christmas had been the worst, he wouldn't let her refuse his kids a proper dinner, never mind he couldn't eat it. He'd been let out the hospital then, even gone down to the pub where someone was quick to report he'd been seen pouring Scotch down his feeding tube just like his bruv had.

What narked everyone was the unfairness of it all. Those beautiful wild boys who'd roused the bar with Springsteen's *The River,* whose raw coarse voices barked at life, whose pontificating about the world in pubs which had changed with posh furniture and food and banning smoking, of all things… Bastard Life had got them all three in the end, in the same way, in the throat.

A Canterbury Tale on a Cockcrow Morning

Patrice and me have got an understanding. I am to write down her story as she speaks. If anyone has a problem with that, tough. Her and her old man often take the train off up to London on a Sunday for a bit of culture. That's if there's no engineering works that is.

So I suppose dat is dat.

Ah nevah tink dis gon happen to me again. If anybody did try and tell me: 'Patrice, when you go out tonite you gon meet the sweetest man and for shame I cyant repeat the things you gon let him do...' I would nevah have believe dem. A grown woman like me! How many times I say – I done finish with white man, they have no regard for my culture? Cheups! Is stupid I stupid or what?

My girlfriends of course had something to say:

'I do hope you realise what you're doing Patrice. Isn't this the sort of behaviour you're always chastising Natasha about?'

(Natasha is her daughter.)

…Jealous fuh true!

Well dat ting just happen so. I only put my head round the dressing-room door to say hi to Neil. Is the first time he put on flamenco at The Penny Theatre and Lawwwdd… I come face to face with Gloriousness. All I can see is Bambi eyes, long hair and big shoulders. Dat was it, chile, dat was IT. He stop strumming dat guitar and he looking and I looking and if I nevah know nuttin 'bout flamenco is know now I know and more besides.

Dere was pure disgust on Janie's and Josene's faces as they left me after the show, heading for the car park with me at the stage door waving!

I dint have to wait long. People still starting dem car when he come strolling out the door with he long legs. He guitar swing over he shoulders. Straight away he fingers grab mine, curl round, lift dem to he mouth. Me heart stop, the first time in a long long night…!

Well the next day I stupid for true. I stand up waiting in Canterbury Cathedral grounds, well at least was before them start charging. Is true dey say more mad people out than in. Is tourist place innit? They swarming like History itself send them. I akse meself is what dey really looking for? You can tell me? Becket to jump out and say Save me! Save me!? Nobody don't look like no pilgrim to me. Only fancy camera and kissmeass rucksack knocking we for hell and go. They know better than akse me for take picture fuh dem!

And all the time I stand up waiting I thinking… Jeez dat man was sweet! Me still shame for tell you! Lift me up naked as the day me born and carry me to the bed. Stupid ole Patrice in hotel bed! At least wasn't one I had to clean! Ha! Just imagine Mr Scott at Reception clocking me as I walking out at dawn hand in hand with one Spanish guitarist hair wild and eyes red like mine. I ought to feel shame. Especially in that holy place where God reading my every thought! *Christ Patrice, I say to myself, you is a wicked woman!*

> I rarely recycle others' thoughts
> My days are a cacophony
> A syrup of languages
> Such cemented histories
> Tales and more tales…
>
> At night, even I sleep. The moon
> Proves a poor companion
> Darkness bends our natures
> To its gloom
>
> Night's bedding down of cities
> Even smothers spires.

You know, dey always used to say me bad. I can still hear Sister Josephine voice, 'That girl has got a brain, but does she use it? No; mixes with all and sundry.'

Lawd, how I was hoping none of Natasha friends pass me waiting like some street woman!

Streetwoman?! I can imagine that chile of mine putting back her head and laughing. 'Christ Mum, what kinda word is that? Anudder funny Caribbean saying?'

Me praise the Lord she was at work. Woulda be the worst ting to pass her own mother waiting for some man in Canterbury Cathedral grounds!

Quando me escharas de menos	Should you miss me
El dia que me esches de menos	On the day you miss me
Le tienes que volver loca	You'll go crazy
Y has de salu a biscarme	And look for me
Como el caballo sin frenos	Like a horse without reins
(Andulusian gypsy song)	

After we had loved for the second time she asked 'why you speak so little?' her words had their own canto, their own rhythm. They dip in and out of this English which she mixes so fast it is sometimes difficult for me to follow. But that was not important, we found other ways of speaking.

She had walked in like rain into the dressing-room. Like the smell before it rains in Andalusia. I had paused my tuning to watch her. Many women come backstage. All over the world it is the same. They all have a hunger underneath the make-up and the little dresses, the tight jeans... I too am guilty. But this one...

There is always a point when I play when I have them under my spell. I could feel their blood rise in the air, a mistral creeping in under the guitar strings. Their feet tap, their fingers beat out the rhythm on the sides of their seats, their eyes flash from me to the guitar. When I stop and they applaud, all their energy fireballs. In that second I raised my head and saw her again. She had risen, just before they all did, but angry. O Madre Mia! Angry like the dancers waiting to enter the dance. I smiled then, I knew I would have her. She knew it too.

You know how the place get full up? Was real commotion y'know, all o' dem people with different accents was like Babel! French students hollering and stuffing dem face with McDonalds, Italians with dem Gucci bags, the South Americans with dem pan pipes, the little nose-ring girl with she *Big Issues*...

But my mind dirty bad! I can't stop thinking of the night jus past, I climbing up the half-light staircase ... man, was just like dem Mills and Boon book I did used to read...!

…panelled dark mahogany. He let her enter first, her feet crossing the short space to the leaded window. She stood there looking down at the street, empty now but for a lone walker who staggered across the precinct. The street lamp gave a yellow tinge to the cobbles and entered the room, resting on the curled knobs of the iron bed, a pale rose on the carpet. She heard him place the guitar against the wall and in the long seconds that his footsteps took to cross the carpet, her heart pounded against her ribs, her hand reaching out to steady herself on the window sill. Cigarette smoke, sandalwood, mint. His thumbs stroked the back of her neck, fingers fanning out over her shoulders, her collar-bone. She turned and traced his face in the half-light, boldly lifted her mouth. His tongue probed hers, fingers forcing passages through her hair. His hair was sleek and damp, his cheekbones high; jolting her into a memory of another time.

('He don't even speak propa English!' Josene had sniggered.)

On Patrice's return one time from the Caribbean, where her tongue had travelled with her sweet full-fat Creole, forgetting to reshape into the Kentish accent, Josene had said. 'You talking really funny Patrice, izzat 'ow they speak in yer country?'

This was a madness. From that one moment in the dressing-room she had remained transfixed: lifting a glass of wine at the bar, listening to him play, Strains of a Spain she knew nothing of induced a pulsing warmth into the cold night, running its fingers along her belly, her legs. Warm as the lip of a calabash pouring river water, sinking onto a sandbank so liquid, her breath broke on a cockcrow morning. He drew her to the bed where she fell, watching his dark hair swing as he removed a white shirt, blue jeans; reminding her again of such hair, such skin and a way of moving that reminded her of salamanders basking in the heat. When he spoke she almost jumped. This was real. His English was precise and matched his movements as he lifted her dress over her head, talking of music and rivers, cupping each breast in turn.

17

In the daylight she laughed at the silliness of it, bit her lip as she leaned on the cloister walls where bright morning light played between the cold stone and the quadrangle expanse of grass.

His fingers had played her just enough for a sharp cry, a stifled outburst of breath, a ripple like a stone across water. She had moved down his body with a soft mouth, a tongue released to curl and curve, conducting currents that made him buck like a canoe on rough water. Sleep had come from somewhere. Bells had rung from somewhere. Morning came.

And then he come nuh! And is then I know I never even notice was brown eyes he had! Christ! Me say to meself, What have I done Lord? But to he me jus say –

'Hi.'

And 'Hey! You okay?'

And me say me fine and he say he sorry he late, he lost, and then me say stupidness: 'It's okay don't worry. Makes a change for me anyway.'

'What make a change?'

And me thinking he smelling nice. Paco Rabanne.

And me rambling: 'Me being here. Never come here usually, you don't when you live in a place do you? Passed out here though.'

Christ what a ranting fool.

'Passed out?' he say, looking at me funny.

'My degree ceremony… hat, gown and li'l ole me, ha ha.'

And me smelling he up and wanting for touch he, looking so nice in he denim shirt and he talking something 'bout – '…Becket at school, Anne Boleyn, Battle of Hastings…'

And I thinking, he remember me climbing 'pon top 'e like a lizard panting? Then I clear me throat and say: 'Dih crypt; leh we head for the crypt. Nice and cool in dere.'

18

Only it come out proper like: 'Would you like to see the crypt? There's tombs and the Reculver pillars…The Black Prince. Remember doing him at school. Didn't mean nothing though! All we ever wanted to do was go out and play!'

'We also. But we travelled, always moving. Playing, singing.'

And when we inside I take him where people light candle and thing: 'You can write a message here, look. People write prayers and put them in the box, see?'

And is just so I find meself you know. To this day me na know why me reach for tha paper and pen and write! And to this day me remember everything, me write:

Dear God, is what am I doing with a Spanish musician on a Saturday morning in this place of holy places? I should be home looking after my daughter and cleaning my house. He is a one-night stand. We both know that. I am a 39 year old has-been with a late degree in a useless subject and I clean hotels. After today I shall never see him again and he will probably never remember me. I have acted like the lowest of sluts and lower still because I enjoyed it so much. I know now what attracted me. He looks a little like my first love who I left for England and no-one has ever come close so am I reliving the past or what? I know it's been a long time since you heard from me but the little convent school girl is still here somewhere so I would really appreciate some guidance at this point. I'm sorry I haven't used this time to pray for peace in the world but I promise I'll light a candle. With reverence, Patrice.

And Felipe took off his hat and smiled. 'Ah Cara, I too remember every word I write that day: *Dear Jesu Christu, is this the woman to stop my wandering? Is this city where my soul will rest? How many more years of women in nightclubs, running angry that my padre say I sell out our gypsy pride?*'

Ah yes; many such wandered
Through my streets
Their carts clattering
Wearing down my stone

The inns were full to the brim
Such a caterwaul!
Those accents from all corners
What a din!

And those minstrels!
The strings of the lute
Pulled many a maid to waken
In the dew of Rough Common
Tales? I've heard them all
From Polperro to Lincoln they roll
Like barrels of ale
Seeking an ear and entry
Into the Kingdom.

Samantha and the Cockerel

Samantha started complaining about the fowl-cock the minute she took up residence in the village. The village, of which we shall name no names, was a spit away from the city, just a twenty minute drive in her 4x4 into the centre and park by the Cathedral walls, or use the Park and Ride if it was Saturday. She and her husband the MP had moved into a new build, an almost authentic-looking country house, far enough from the riff-raff, the dossers on the street, the louts at the bus stop and the yobbos out at the weekend. The village was used to being a holding centre for the town come to countries. The original cottages had been bought up, knocked through and out and up as far as the council would allow, and larger, newer builds were creeping over every little spare ground, replacing and converting barns and disused churches, offering four bedrooms, sweeping drives, landscaped gardens and summerhouses. I tell you child, was up you were going in the world if you could find the money for one of those! And it was to one such that she came, a model-turned actress from somewhere east of the Thames, who wasn't lucky so much in its true sense as one who forced luck to come her way. And luck, which in this instance meant a man with money, was wheedled into her turquoise gaze like a fisherman fighting a large tuna, and caught in such a comfortable hue, happily stayed, although fighting on a daily basis for a comfortable quality of air.

Samantha was one of those rare creatures who knew exactly what she wanted. Country life was Hunter wellies, a designer kitchen, Cath Kidston tea towels, a range, and large rooms overlooking fields. She did not however want mud on the tiles, any odour that remotely resembled fertiliser, and certainly not a blasted cockerel strutting himself not only at dawn, but at any old time of the day or night. Her beautiful turquoise eyes narrowed the moment Percival crowed, for that was the cockerel's name, Percival from over the road owned by someone described by Samantha as 'the dippy woman with cats', who also owned a horse, two sheep and Percival's many wives and daughters. Samantha, deciding that she quite liked it here for the moment, loving her house and its gabled roofs which no-one would have known were not 16th Century, tried the direct approach and turned up on Dippy's rustic front door not many weeks after she had moved in. 'I do hope we're not going to fall out about this,' she told Dippy, her smile warm under the coral lip-gloss, 'but it isn't as if it's only once a day is it? I may have been able to put up with that, after all...' (here she paused briefly, drew her gaze across the surrounding rural vista, and breathed in deeply), 'but it's really quite un-nerving all hours of the day and night. You must find it disconcerting yourself,' she added kindly, 'we all came here for the peace and quiet after all, so would you consider letting him go?'

Two of Percival's wives had settled around Dippy's feet, knowing she carried the odd treat in her pockets; they both cocked their heads up at Turquoise Eyes at this moment, then swiftly up at Dippy as if seeking reassurance.

'Percival lives 'ere and 'eel die 'ere,' Dippy said, and promptly shut the door. She promptly opened it again. 'There are those of us who 'ave lived and died here too,' she snapped and shut the door again.

Samantha was momentarily taken aback at the cheek, the cheek. No-one interacted with her on that level. Goodness.

She marched back across the road, up the driveway, fully aware of Percival's red comb fluttering away on the gate post. She smoothed her perfectly flat stomach as her Hunter wellies scrunched the gravel.

Him who paid the bills had his ear bent that night, and the next, and the next. He was a Liberal and tried his best to live up to his principles but he was also in the running for the European Parliament and really couldn't be having this sort of … ripple in his otherwise ambitious life. He looked at his lovely wife over the Merlot.

'Darling we have to live and let live, this *is* the country after all. Perhaps it was all a bit too much too soon aye? Are you missing London, truly?'

His wife banged the silver down on the oak. 'Don't patronise me Gareth. We're not actually living in a farmyard are we?'

Gareth did look, had looked, had allowed her free rein with hours on the internet looking at houses and traipsing down here on the Highspeed which wasn't actually highspeed you know, after Ashford. Perhaps that was something he could bring to the Parliament table … Big Business and the Trade Descriptions Act…

'You're not listening are you?! You'll have to have a

word with her!'

'A word? Whatever for?' He drained the wine glass and stood up. 'Look darling, I have some papers to look at. Good dinner, MasterChef as usual.'

Samantha fumed. Slammed the dishwasher. Sprayed Cillit Bang furiously around the splashback, polished the Corian worktop to a shine. Over the fence Percival stretched his wings out, put his head back and crowed.

She rang the Council. A sympathetic but tired-sounding woman took her details and promised to look into it. In the meantime Samantha tried to get on with her new life, getting decorators in, having friends come down from London. Balanced the signed copy of Nigella's latest on the white wrought-iron recipe-book holder, and prepared Gareth the most luscious of meals. She began to recognise that there was actually a pattern to Percival's crowing. Each dawn, each mid-morning, each tea-time and dusk his proclamation to his mistresses and the sky pierced through her sleep, her telephone calls, the drilling from the plumber, and Jeremy Vine's radio show. She even tried phoning Jeremy Vine, where after being directed to the website a researcher politely took her details and thanked her for her call and said they had recently covered a discussion about townies in the country, so sorry. She phoned the Council again who asked who it was she had spoken to and promised eagerly to do his utmost in his young jerky voice. Gareth came and went, stroking her perfectly flat stomach on the evenings he wasn't too tired and began to make murmurings about children.

Her mother and sister came down for the weekend exclaiming at how much she'd done already and what was it like living here really and didn't she miss her friends? It was the Monday after they'd left, driving off in the old Volvo that reminded her so much of Daddy, that, after she had just shut the door, was surprised to hear a furious banging on her beautiful oak front door that had only just been varnished. She opened it at speed, to see a fist half-raised in the air. It was the weirdo from across the road.

Samantha blinked. 'Excuse me…?'

'I'll effing excuse *you* more like! Who the blinkin' 'ell do you think you are sending the Council on me? Do you know how many years us has lived 'ere?'

'The Council? Oh they've been to see you have they?' Despite a little bit of trepidation at this vile creature in her Primark jumper and in what looked like track bottoms for goodness sake, Samantha did feel a little smug. She crossed her arms and looked down at the woman's un-conditioned grey head.

'I did ask you nicely to get rid of that…'

A finger was furiously waved in her face.

'My Percival and me have been together ten year, ten year. And 'is father before him and '*is* father before 'im…'

'Oh really, you're into ancestry are you?'

'…Don't you eff me about with yer fancy talk! You wanna fight on yer 'ands? You got one!'

So saying she marched off down the gravel driveway in her trainers.

Samantha closed the door and took a deep breath. What a nasty encounter. Wait till she told Gareth.

'You did what!' Gareth stepped back and looked at the wife whose beauty had knocked him sideways since she been Miss East England.

'You called the Council on someone who has lived here all her life? Because of a bloody chicken!'

Samantha blinked, and blinked again. A tear wound its lonely way from the turquoise eyes over the smooth cheek. Was this her Gareth not defending her? Oh my.

'Perhaps you could apologise. And get a job or have a baby or something for Christ sake. How on earth am I going to get a seat in Europe if a whiff of this comes out?'

Samantha was mortified. Were those really her choices to circumnavigate the current situation? She examined her sleek silhouette in the hallway mirror, running her palms over her stomach, and imagining a baby growing there, pumping it up like a bicycle tyre. The thought quite disgusted her. A job then; go out and scrabble around to be noticed as she'd done for the past ten years? She'd done her jobbing; all those lunches with ugly men, and parading up catwalks in cold Blackpool. Marriage to Gareth was the payoff, the reward. In some respects she had a job anyway, looking after Gareth and the house, not even having a housekeeper. She quite liked running the Dyson over the carpet from Fenwicks, and loading the black shiny Bosch dishwasher. Liked putting on those Laura Ashley washing-up gloves and washing the beautiful Portuguese tiles. She was an artist, creating a House Beautiful, a setting for Gareth and his political people. You had to have some idea of style to select curtain material and soft furnishings. She'd been thinking of getting *Homes and Gardens* in for an interview when the house was finished. That'd make them sit up and take notice! It didn't matter that she wasn't as intellectual as Gareth either, they were all so full of talk themselves; eye candy was all they wanted. She sighed; maybe she could get involved in charitable things.

But she was diverting: the problem of Percival was what they – she – was supposed to be sorting. Samantha looked out of her wide bay windows that overlooked the sloping lawn. For the first time she wondered about her other neighbours. She hadn't taken much notice being so busy with the house, apart from next door who drove a soft-top mini and was hardly there, she didn't know anything about anyone. Maybe she should get the gang on her side, so to speak, if Dippy was going to get nasty.

The next morning Samantha did what she hardly ever did, went for a walk. But the walk did have purpose, she needed to see who lived where and did what. But walking casually along a country road whose drives disappeared anonymously behind hedges didn't tell her anything. She did catch sight of one or two heads doing gardening things. She didn't realise it was such a long lane; lanes were longer when you walked. What had been a selling point of their house seemed rather tedious now. Her legs were beginning to ache. The old cottages appeared, a row on either side of the main road, once farm cottages, she guessed, now done up quite nicely with new windows and things. There was actually a human being also, painting an iron gate. He looked up as she approached.

'Morning.'

'Good morning…'

She paused. But before she could enlarge on the greeting, he nodded and disappeared up his garden path. She looked ahead. Wasn't there a shop here somewhere? She distinctly remembered her and Gareth making jokes about having somewhere to go when they ran out of wine. As if. She did almost everything online. But here she was now, and weren't village shops supposed to be friendly and helpful? She read the sign above the door. *Proprietor Mrs Shanti Singh.*

A bell rang as she entered. A quick glance around told her they sold newspapers, sweets, and things you might just run out of, like soup, orange squash and sliced bread. And eggs. Proudly displayed in a pretty basket with the label 'Locally Laid'.

'May I help you?' A tiny, but beautiful Indian woman appeared from the back of the shop. She was wearing a green and lemon sari and gold earrings in the shape of peacocks. Was that real turquoise? Goodness. Samantha blinked.

'Are you new here?' The beautiful woman smiled with graciousness.

' I, I … yes we live at The Paddocks, I was just getting my bearings…'

'Ahh! The Paddocks, yes, Dorothy said she'd had new neighbours.'

'Dorothy?'

She pointed at the eggs…

The free local paper lay spread open on the oak table. Both Gareth and Samantha were temporarily speechless. There on the front page the blaring headlines:

MP's Wife Attacks Local Woman

Beneath the photograph of Dippy looking hurt, with Percival in her arms, his red comb resting on her bosom, the words in smaller print:

Local charity worker Dorothy Ward with Percival, her prize cockerel, winner three times Best of Breed.

"I couldn't believe it", Miss Ward said, "I've lived here all my life in this village, my father farmed sheep and cows until the Government European Policies made him lose his livelihood. All I have now is a few animals, with the sale of eggs helping me get by. Percival keeps the hens happy, without his presence they wouldn't lay as well."

Mrs Gareth Finlay-Smythe, a former beauty queen and model from Essex, married to one of the rising political stars, is said to have reported Miss Ward to the council because she objected to Percival's crowing. "They've said that any objections by neighbours could lead to the removal of all my layers," Miss Ward added tearfully.

This newspaper is dedicated to highlight the concerns of local people. Is this the new society we're heading for? Are we going back to the days of landowners and tyrants?

Gareth paced the living–room with his hands in his pockets. He stiffened his shoulders before heading for the front door.

'Gareth! Where are you…?'

Samantha looked open-mouthed as the man who professed to love her made off in the direction of the enemy. What on earth…?

She stood at the open front door and waited. And waited. For some reason her thoughts turned to her Daddy. Poor Daddy who'd have been so proud to have seen her now. Seen her 'make it'. Daddy wouldn't have liked to see his Sammy's lip trembling though. What did he used to say? 'Beat the buggers at their own game.'

Half an hour later Gareth was back with a box of eggs: large, brown, with feathers still on them. He stood back with a self-contented smile.

Samantha looked down at the eggs, then at Gareth, who was saying something she closed her ears to.

Beat 'em at their own game.

For some reason that Singh lady's earrings popped into her mind. And Samantha knew straight away what she was going to do.

Peacocks.

She could see them now, gracing her front lawn, and the photo spread in *Homes and Gardens*…

Through the kitchen window Percival's lunch-time chorus pierced the air like an Angelus bell.

…and not only more beautiful but louder than *you, Cock.*

The Secret Life of Alphonso

What some people don't understand is that dogs understand virtually everything you say. I'm not talking about the basics, the Sit, Come and Drop instructions. I'm talking about proper conversation, with all its hidden under-currents. The only reason they don't join in is because they don't choose to; it's much more productive to use their emotional eyes or whimper.

Alphonso could tell you chapter and verse if he chose to, or epistle and gospel as Gran used to say. He could tell you about the woodland cottage in Wales where he lived happily and relatively freely for the first two years of his life. He could tell you of the sheer and utter pleasure of sailing over the bank and into the Teifi River with all the abandon a Springer spaniel is known for; he could tell you of his helicopter landings, and un-measurable thrill of the morning with its birdsong and constant mud-smell rain, and the persistent and unfortunately never-fulfilled desire of getting his teeth round a cat.

There was only one ripple in the calm water of Alphonso's life, his owners. Like all children, Alphonso grew up loving these substitute parents, but with only the barest memory of his mother, a memory contained within the remnants of his blanket. Don't get me wrong, his owners loved him to bits, spoilt and disciplined him in equal contradiction between their love for him and the rules of his dog training classes. With the battle of the sofa won, and the biscuit treat never denied, the one complaint was that his owners did not seem to love each other as much as they loved him, they argued and argued about returning to the city and unfortunately things got to the point where before he knew it, they were driving a hired van up the M4 with all their possessions in the back.

Which is why Alphonso now officially resides at Number 4 Chapel Walk, Canterbury; an apartment with a balcony from which Alphonso looked down with complete and utter disdain on something called a river. With the waterfalls of Penbryn and Cenarth still in his mind, this gentle ribbon of water bearing groups of smiling passengers up and down its tame length, appeared to him the height of utter banality.

His owners were trying to make a new life for themselves, and had established for Alphonso a pattern of early morning and late walks around Solly's Orchard, a square of green in Canterbury's City Centre which Alphonso reluctantly appreciated, given its historical significance, a little patch of country in the city, with those lovely apple trees planted by the council in 2007 and given names like Eden and Harvest Festival, lovely to cock your leg up on. His owners themselves seemed to have been given a new lease of life and were out and about daily, immersing themselves in the cultural life of the city. Life having lost its edge, from the balcony Alphonso whined with no achievable results.

Much is said about a dog's power of scent, and soon Alphonso had come to know the scents of Solly's Orchard intimately; from the treaded-in footprints of residents and visitors and the litter of last night's chips, to the unique and individual smells of other dogs, dogs for whom Alphonso could not bring himself to respect, due to their dull eyes and soft paws.

When four lunging legs and two flapping ears sailed past him on a dry and bright spring morning, racing away from her owner and plunging into the river, Alphonso's nose, ears and eyes were electrified into existence. He recognised the breed as an Italian Spinone, having already met one back in his dog training classes back in Wales. Alphonso remembered his owners making quite a fuss of that one, and they had looked back at Alphonso with a wistful expression on their faces. The owner of this one was a mangy looking girl with legs like a colt wearing something like Joseph's Technicolour Dream-Coat (which Alphonso had watched on TV). She was shouting HERA! at the top of her voice, to which Hera did not respond, but was immersed at the upper end of the weir opposite the Millers Arms. Alphonso's interest was stimulated to the point of such strength and excitability that he slipped his lead and found himself racing after Hera with a speed he had not employed since Cardigan Bay. He flung himself into the water with all the grace of a stampeding hippo circling, swimming, splashing, licking and frolicking.

Hera took to her reprobate companion with instant and uninhibited bliss, together they frothed the waters of the weir into something resembling a jacuzzi. Passers-by, unused to such frenetic activity on a usually dignified morning, stood and stared. Both owners, at first frozen inactive, began to combine the use of their voices to the best of their ability, an action that was totally disregarded, pre-empting the unusual and reportable action of them having to step into the water themselves to retrieve their dogs. The slippery, almost unachievable act took several minutes, and when eventually successful, both owners were so angry with their dogs they barely had time to communicate with each other. Alphonso, returned to his true nature, fought the lead all the way back to Number 4 Chapel Walk.

The words of condemnation, and the confinement to his basket all that day did nothing to stem Alphonso's gloom; he was not happy with his new life, and intended to do something about it.

The advantage of having a balcony is that it is a place to watch the world go by. It is also a platform. Alphonso knew where his proverbial bread was buttered, so he did not want to turn his back on that basic need. He also did honestly love his owners. But a dog has to do what a dog has to do, and Alphonso decided to do what his owners themselves had done: compromise.

To this end, Alphonso plotted his secret life, one which to this day he is living. Each day when his owners go out, Alphonso sails over the balcony (some ten feet) into the river. He has a swim, shakes himself and takes himself for a walk. At times his owners will hear reports that someone saw Alphonso outside the NatWest Bank with the buskers, nudging coins into flat caps and open guitar cases. They say they saw Alphonso in Dane John Gardens with the girl with the Italian Spinone. They say even he was spotted ambling around the Sturry Marshes. His owners do not believe this. They leave Alphonso in his basket every day and he is there when they return. Besides how would he get out, or get back in?

Only Alphonso knows the truth. And he's not telling.

Guitar Hero

Carissa has been singing and dancing since before she could walk. Carissa's daddy was around then, when the thrill of being a baby father was the business, and any little deal he had going down was weaved in around playing her each new track hot off the press or sitting them in front the telly watching MTV. That man, a pretty man too, by all accounts, lived for music the way some people lived for alcohol, or gastronomic delights, and played a mean guitar. Carissa knew Bo Diddley by the time she was two, she gave three-year old impressions of Hendrix doing *All Along the Watchtower*, she could copy J.Lo to a T, Madonna to a D for Diva. Her tiny trebly voice boomed out of the karaoke machine by the time she was four and sometime around then is when her daddy slid out the door.

Carissa's mother Amber was not what you thought of as a victim. After dissing the man every opportunity she had, and wiping the slate clean of any mutual friends who still spoke to him, she decided to change her life completely and moved to Canterbury. She found herself a job, made new friends, and clubbed when she could afford it.

For Carissa the hours in front of MTV came to an end, as did the weekly thrill of playing new sounds her daddy got hot off the press; or listening to her daddy play his guitar. Amber just listened to Invicta and sometimes Radio Kent as a backdrop to her constant phone calls whilst she stirred dinner, painted her nails, and ran baths for her little woman who had started school by now and needed regularity. But the dancing and the singing in Carissa kept living. The child used a hairbrush for a mike, hummed still-remembered riffs from Hendrix, which she played with fingers growing long and decorated in the glowing colours belonging to her mother. Amber enrolled her into ballet school.

'She don't get it from me!', Amber would guffaw to some girlfriend or relation visiting who watched Carissa do her air guitar and dance like a four-foot diva on the laminate floor. 'Um ummm!' said company would expel, 'I never seen the like! Where this chile get her thing from!?'

They still talked their home-talk, these black women, who had sniffed at Amber's decision to leave Peckham at first as a betrayal and then in admiration. 'Nuff time to leave the bastard city, best for the chile, but not many black faces round 'ere, you don't feel outaplace chile?' Amber had done her own sniffing and quipped that since when does black people not feel outaplace anywhere in the world and only one generation back was the banana boat but they has got to take the lead from the poet Grace Nichols when she say 'Anywhere I hang my knickers is my home'.

Those who had had some acquaintance with the baby father would roll their eyes and say, 'Well it look like he leave something positive in the chile!'

By this time Amber had settled down nicely with a guy called Francis, with a dependable job at a well-known supermarket chain, with opportunity to progress to Store Manager. Taking on a woman with a child was not something easily done, but Francis had already sown his wild oats, and had been a very young baby father himself, a shock, which at sixteen had had the wonderful effect of straightening out any kinks in his character, setting him on the right path, and even supporting his son whom many had remarked looked every inch of his baby mother. There was no Carissa's daddy to contend with, so Francis had slid more or less smoothly into life with Amber, paying the bills, going out now and then, and having friends over for dinner.

The summer Carissa was twelve she rebelled. Cute Carissa became moody Carissa who didn't want no man who was not her daddy telling her what to do. There was things and things Carissa told neither her mother nor Francis. School was a war-zone she'd had to fight in since the age of ten; it only took one sour-face girl to repeat some racist slur she'd heard to send feathers flying in the playground. Carissa got sharp, empowered by snippets of black literature touched on in school, Rosa Parks and Martin Luther; and music of course. It was a good time to be black when the charts were full of artists like Jay-Z, Beyoncé, JLS and Rihanna. So the girl found her world and carved her place in it, supported in the sidelines by the powerful, raucous women who were her mother and her mother's friends. The girl had friends too, how good or how bad they were always remains to be seen. But still, in the pit of Carissa's heart was a big big hole, and the only thing that could really fill it was her dancing.

Somehow school began to lose its flavour, then she wasn't really into ballet, street dance was more her thing, and the clothes she began to wear turned Amber's face to stone. The friends she brought home (when she did, as the streets were the new front room) hung their mean faces low and dull as the gum they chewed with a brief 'awright?' at Amber. Francis' hard-earned wages had helped to install Sky so the music videos were turned up loud and filled with the gyrating pelvises of young girls who looked like hookers and guys with their waxed chests and supercilious jaw-lines looking both murderously and lovingly at their women. Mornings were battlegrounds of whipped sheets and slamming doors. After long stretches of altercation and interaction between well-meaning authorities, the next shock for Amber was answering her door one Saturday morning to a long thin man who turned out to be Carissa's baby father.

'Leon? Leon!'

He leaned against the doorframe and watched her before saying, in a well-rehearsed manner, sorry for the surprise and the long time out of touch but life had taken him in directions he had been forced to follow and only the Almighty had lighted the way out of despair and the pits of hell and the biggest loss had been lack of communication with his beloved daughter Carissa for which he was duly absolutely and unquestionably deeply profoundly sorry and if he was to be given another chance neither Amber nor Carissa would regret it, and by the way he had every respect for Francis, the man, the brother, the new anointed, whom the sisters had informed him was due respect.

For one brief moment in his tamarind eyes Amber saw the young man in whom her unformed self had almost drowned its spirit. She saw the locks he'd begun to grow when Carissa was born (not strictly partial to the Rastafarian faith but as a symbol of new life in all its creative power) tumble out of the tam as he stood hat in hand at her front door. She saw the sideways smile that had used to kill her dead in those early dancehall days whilst she and her girlfriends pushed their way to the very front of the stage deafened by the big speakers. She saw his hands with the long fingers and the onyx ring cupping their baby girl onto his lap with the feeding bottle. And then she saw the weeks of Carissa screaming cos her daddy had gone. Bile rose straight out of her liver and became an ejaculation of words.

He stood still waiting.

When she had done, her heart beating loud and fast, and words like *waste of space* and *useless inconsiderate hard-hearted mean bastard* danced around the doorway like angry slashes of light, he raised his head and said quietly 'Can I come in now?'

Carissa meantime was in Essex (unbeknown to her mother). She was dressed in lime-green hot-pants with black lace tights, red stilettos borrowed from her friend Hayley's big sister (unbeknown to *her*) a black basque and a black leather jacket with a faux-fur hood. She stood outside a driveway with Hayley and a dozen or so other girls dressed in a range of attire that stretched from diamanté hoods to brief skirts that dared the cold. The golden portal at the end of the driveway was a garage door, guarded by four or five young men who smoked weed and laughed, gold glinting from wrists and fingers. Occasionally the doors opened, and through the haze of pungent smoke and the dull boom of music a finger would beckon and the guard-dogs parted to let a couple of the girls in. With a rush they would all surge forward, only to be held back by the snarling toughies who gave the impression of being charming, and who could easily give you the nod if they liked your style. With the jostling of breasts, compost of perfumes, the familiarity and high fives, it was quite apparent that having an asset was the key. Carissa stepped back and eyed up her opponents. No-one there would know she was only thirteen. All of them were high style. Big eyes, false eyelashes, bright mouths and hair that had taken hours, days, months to weave, colour, shape and pay for. She watched one of them stroke the tattooed arm of the tall guy. Another pursed her bronze lips against the cheek of the stubbled one. For all her mouth and attitude, Carissa recoiled. She stood apart and closed her eyes. She could feel the beat through the doors and the concrete floor. So she danced. She'd come here to dance, so that's what she did. She was Beyoncé, she was J.Lo, she was Christina Aguilera. She was Madonna in the eighties. Lady Gaga had nothing on her. She was in her own wild world on this universe of concrete where dreams stoked rough rhythms banging out the garage doors. Snakes hissed their spite from lipstick mouths as the other girls clocked her. But then, 'little darling!' an oiled voice ran. And she opened her eyes to find her arm guided by one of the guards who locked eyes with her, and drew her against the wall.

'Sweet sugar, how come I ain't seen you nowhere?'

And she shrugged and replied, 'Oh, I been around.'

And stole the chance and said, 'You think you could get me in?'

And he sucked in his cheeks and whistled, his thumb lifting her chin.

'Dixie is a busy man!' He swept his fingers in the direction of the driveway where the queue had grown even longer. 'And we don't know nuttin 'bout you sweetness. More than our job's worth to let just any little girl in here now. We're dealin' with the main man here.'

'I don't know you either, and I just want to dance.'

'Um hmmn, everybody want to dance, sweetness. But they got pass by me now.' He laughed. 'They call me the Gatekeeper you know.'

Carissa felt the eyes of the other girls pouring down on her with scorn. She thought of her mother slagging her off this morning about another meeting up the school.

Same time, back in Canterbury, her long lost daddy was saying to her cold mother, 'Don't say nuttin; I can surprise her.'

He stretched his long legs out and checked out his baby mother's living-room. Leather sofa, laminate floor, African rug. Nice. Hadn't quite sold out to Mammon then. Francis had come home from work and after the shock of seeing Carissa's blood-father had held his tongue and decided to be civil. He had his universe to protect, and in his experience it was wise to use the lessons of some of the African folk tales he had been brought up with. Anansi the spider never openly confronted his enemy; instead he buttered him up with sweet talk and compliments, so distracting his opponent who could be any creature from a snake to a jaguar. Leon was playing the part of the Born Again, dropping the name of the Almighty into every phrase, re-iterating time and again his sinfulness at being a bad father, the lost sheep. Epiphany had come through a not-surprising prison sentence, little bits of this and little bits of that, and the small matter of downloading music illegally and selling this and that on. He peppered his language with a blend of Old Testament Rastafarianisms, referring both to *Jah* and The Lord; and seeing himself in the role of Abraham, tested to sacrifice his son *hic* daughter. 'True is the Light of the Lord Almighty,' he said, 'that he should take their daughter out of Babylon into the Promised Land!' Francis found his metaphors a bit confusing, but held his tongue.

Carissa did not come home. After checking with all of her friends whom Amber had numbers for, Amber practised the well-known and justifiable act of checking her daughter's Facebook account. She had managed to crack her password just recently, ready for an occasion just like this. And there it was. *Checking in for the video audition for Dixie Dreadman! Me and Hay!* But there was no address, just those one-line answers the kids use: *Cool Man! Rock it! Up there with the bitches man!* And the like.

Leon, walking into a situation for which he was totally unprepared, and unable to criticise the parental control of his one and only daughter by the people who had been raising her all this time, remembered his oath of allegiance to the law of the Born Again. He also remembered that of all the people who would know what music action was going down and where it was, it was him, and in ten minutes, through the double action of using his iPhone and Facebook, he tracked Dreadman and the address of the audition. Without further ado, he offered the services of his chariot, a recently acquired souped-up Mazda, the sight of which raised Amber's eyebrows and caused a normally non-West Indian Francis to suck his teeth, and soon they were driving at manageable speed along the M2. During the charge of the posse, to pass the time and ease the worry, the peoples had to talk, and so Leon learned of the new hard times with Carissa, and so Amber and Francis were treated to the wishes and dreams of a Leon who, wanting to re-connect with his daughter, was also investigating the possibility of opening a li'l place somewhere close by where the young people could come and do their thing. Amber spent a lot of the journey with her lips pursed and looking out the window. But by and by, in little more than an hour, they exited the Dartford Tunnel. Traffic slowed them up on that side of the Thames, but eventually they made their way off the motorway, turned off down B roads and nosed into a side street of unpretentious looking terraced houses. Girls clad in the fashions already described, were disconsolately coming out in twos and threes from a wide driveway at the end of the road. Leon didn't look to see if parking was legal, Amber didn't hesitate approaching one of the disappointed girls, and Francis and Leon soon time approached the Gatekeeper with long legs and determined strides. At this point Francis, it must be said, did hold back; with his short clipped hair and work suit he did look a tad out of place. Leon, however, did the guy thing. The fist-shake, the smile, the whisper to the Gatekeeper, and lo and behold the doors opened like the parting of the waters.

The auditions were coming to a close. Guys were packing up recording equipment, winding up cables and cameras. A sound-track was winding down. Through the smoky air a cluster of girls were head to head with a guy whom the Gatekeeper indicated was the main man. Naturally Leon did not know his daughter. But Amber, in that lioness way that some mothers have, marched her through the scent of weed and perfume, and up to the caricature of her daughter and without further ado grabbed her by the arm to face her. Carissa's face was a picture. Her mother, in the way that some mothers have, loving in the midst of anger, pulled her close to her chest, and only then did she turn her to face the man standing behind her, whose face ran the gamut of emotions, with tears not far away.

Carissa said two words: 'Holy' and 'Shit'.

I won't tell a lie and say that things all went smoothly after that. Once a leopard always a leopard, but even they have to slow up sometimes. Leon did get his little business going; in these internet days Canterbury was as good as anywhere. I won't say that Carissa became some angel overnight, or that there weren't rucks between the mother, father and stepfather, or that Carissa didn't use her cards to suit herself and played boomerang between them all. But she is going back to school, she is still singing and dancing, and everybody trying to work things out. You can't say fairer than that.

Dawn Chorus

There's a good bus service from Canterbury to Folkestone: numbers 16 and 17, once they clear the city is a lovely drive through the countryside through villages like Barham and Hawkinge. Me with my straying, I frequently encounter fellow aliens like myself; we all have the one thing in common – once we get through that English habit of not talking to strangers is talk we talk. So that's how I met Savitree who'd been married to a Nepalese unfortunately blown up in Afghanistan.

Savitree's circumstances had lowered her to take a cleaning job, and during the week she worked for a company called Mandy's Fresh 'n Kleen who cleaned offices and factories, and sometimes churches. It was on a Friday morning she first felt the presence, she told me.

'I feel like was somebody watching me,' she confessed.

He watched her as she cleaned. Her small frame had now

learnt to manoeuvre the big machine, the muscles on her neck taut. She was still shivering; always took her a while to warm up, would walk in rubbing her arms no matter what time of year it was. The nature of the job being what it was, it was always dawn. In the midst of the group whose chattering he liked to describe as a new dawn chorus, she was the quiet one. He suspected that some of them had come from warmer climes originally, although he picked up some smatterings of European languages, from countries which he wouldn't have an inkling what they were called now, with all the drawing and re-drawing of borders through the centuries. They all brought shadows with them.

The cleaning machine purred over the floors; for such a big machine it really didn't make much noise at all. The machine rolled over stone and wood, rubber and tile.

The crypt was her patch. Whether by choice or order who knows? It wasn't the choice of some, he knew that. He listened to the comments: 'Not me, down there with those ghosts!' The others preferred the bright chapel with its colourful stained glass windows, the sacristy with its marble altar, the pews over which yellow chamois flicked and danced. Just as well it wasn't those Romans with all their statues and fanciful pictures.

In the crypt the little woman circled the Black Knight; her heart, as usual, beating just that little bit faster. Part of her believed he was still there under that stone mask. She couldn't get her head round entombing, coming from a culture where they burned their dead, giving them the distinction of purification, accompanying them to the fire with ululations and lamentations, setting their souls free with the flame. But it was not right to criticise. What sufferings were her people now going through, despite all their belief in the order of life? She closed her eyes and leaned temporarily on the cleaner. *I am blessed. I am blessed.* And chanted a mantra for the transformation of her husband's soul into a life more blessed than this one had been.

He sighed as he heard her mantra. Soon she would do what she always did, head for the prayer corner, look around surreptitiously, hastily write something on the yellow slip of paper provided and drop into the box. Light a candle.

Learned as time had made him, European languages were all he could read… what she wrote was one of those other languages that were more symbols than letters, although he mused, aren't letters symbols? She also wrote from right to left. Her olive skin didn't tell you anything, and she wore a puffa jacket and trainers just like the others.

When he could stir himself, he could see out and over the city wall, see the groups waiting, the unending caterpillar of buses crawl in and out of the bus station. He read the names on the front to keep himself up to scratch, Hawkinge, Barham, Elham; remembered stories of others who had streamed in from those places weary from the journey, on horseback, foot or carriage. He enjoyed the little scenarios outside the walls, the lover waiting, the woman looking anxiously at her watch, the businessmen almost running, man-bags slapping their thighs. He often wondered what the hurry was for most of them: living as long as he had, time didn't have the urgency for him as it does for so many. Maybe that's why he enjoyed with a sacrilegious fervour the bad behaviour of the young people, relished the loud shrieks of laughter at school-times, the jostling at the bus-stop, the shoving off the pavements. He loved their raw vicious energy, the well-worn Anglo-Saxon phrases that depended on their horror of their bodily functions. He was pleased he was still able to adapt and enjoy this wonderful rich English language, this organically growing bastard child of conquerors and peasants. How many centuries had they all thronged here in sandalled, bare and leathered feet, sackcloth, chamois, felt, cotton, twill? How many euphemisms had bounced off these hallowed walls, how many Pentecostal tongues, Cromwellian bare-boned throats, French, Greek, Spanish, American, inflections? His bones were hollowed elephant tusks, they were flute and timpani, crochet, quaver, slang, rhythm and blues. *Is all rite, innit?*

He was proud of his capabilities.

He loved the rush of young tourists in the summer, smiled to himself as their leaders attempted to point out the cultural significance of what they were being treated to. Data, dates, bronze, pews, architecture. Beneath full view they charged like beagles out on the hunt, swinging their rucksacks against the freedomed bones and loins of young girls in tight blue jeans. Hallelujah. Their texting fingers were as fleet as mosquitos in the rain. Their laughter like the barking of young wolf cubs.

The older ones now; dressed in the clothes of their culture, walking slowly along the city streets, the men with their hands behind their backs. They stared in the shop windows, went into the pound shops. Waited at the bus station with carrier bags from Wilkinsons.

The little woman put her hands together at her forehead and bowed, backing away to where she had left the cleaning machine.

He yawned. One of these days he might just play a little trick on her. Speak possibly.

Savitree leaned close to me on the bus.

'Is like I know what he's thinking,' she said. 'And I tell you what he did last week, he blew my candle out. For true.'

This Mother Country Business

I came to this country in 1953. Right country come to town I was then! A mere boy, a skinny brown-skin boy with blue eyes. They didn't know what to make of me!

Walked up and down the streets of Walthamstow with an address from my old Pa in my hand. He was an Englishman you know, oh yes, through and through. Went to the West Indies in 1930 and never came back. Married my Ma, a coloured woman, and lived like a native. Except for the club of course. Always went to the club!

Up and down I walked.

'Sorry love, don't know.' 'Sorry mate, never heard of it.' Even the British bobby shook his head, eyeing my brown suit and Pa's ancient suitcase suspiciously. Might have thought I had a body in it! But he pointed me to the Y, where an old crone in pink overalls and matching lips led me up narrow stairs with dark green walls going round and round forever. By the time I got to know my way about, the address was long lost, maybe slipped through some crack on that mantelpiece with the wage slips and bus tickets…! Pa could have got it wrong anyway. Any relations he might have had must have been dead and buried long ago.

But I met my lovely wife Joycelyn in the end, and thirty-five years we were married, thirty-five … all fine, until she got ill of course, and then that letter came…

'Eliot, there is a letter here from Guyana.'

I was getting ready for work, feeling in my coat pocket for my keys. Then remembering, she'd borrowed the car to go to the hospital the night before. I remember looking up as she came in with the milk.

'Where did you put my keys last night?'

'I said there's a letter here for you from Guyana!'

'How can there be?' I said. 'I don't know anybody there anymore.'

She looked at me the way she did when denying our dog Sam another biscuit. One of her eyebrows lifted and stayed there.

'Well, this is a Guyana stamp and I think this is your name, Mr E.D. Graham…'

I took it from her. She was right. The long black sprawl of a fountain pen on a brown envelope. Who could it be? Mother and Pa were dead and buried years now and all that business with the probate and insurance had eventually ground to a halt. I thrust the letter into my pocket, cross.

Joycelyn lifted my keys off the window sill and I kissed her on her cheek.

The car took some starting that morning. I remember scraping ice off the windscreen, the engine struggling into life, backing out carefully through the gateway that Joycelyn opened for me every morning.

The headmaster's Ford opposite eased out and I let him turn into the road first; a man should be able to get along with his neighbours. It takes a long time to build up respect, you know. It was a nice area, with an avenue of leylandii and detached bungalows with open front gardens.

I remember thinking: we could have done worse than move here. I was happy as I turned out into the lane, cruising between the fields of winter cabbage and the still-green orchard of apple trees. I passed the oast-house and saw a 'Sold' sign and remember thinking, thank Christ. The place had been getting to be a bit of an eyesore. We had heard some developer had bought it. I drove past the village green, the Dog and Duck, the 16th Century church we attended on Sundays. The butcher's shop was already open, and half of a sheep's carcass was going through the door.

I had liked the oldness of the place from the start, but of course modernity was creeping in, old buildings transformed below into banks and building societies, charity and betting shops. Parents and school-children were waiting fretfully by the zebra crossing, and some old soul held up the proceedings as her shopping trolley refused to leave the pavement! As the lights changed, two teenage girls, long hair flying, dashed through the moving traffic. Ah yes, I remember thinking how I wasn't one bit sorry I and Joycelyn had not had any children!

At work I noted my nameplate on the grey car park wall with pleasure, 'E.D. Graham, Assistant Manager'. I felt I deserved every metal letter etched into that plate. All those years after walking so many of Walthamstow's streets with a non-existent address in my hand!

In my office a surprising sun entered through the opened blinds, spreading itself across my desk and washing the weekend out of dark corners. With all the cutbacks the cleaner only came once a week and on the filing cabinet dust and crumbs of compost from the plant pots held my attention for a minute before I started pulling the drawers out, scanning the layout of accounts and policies. It was then my Mother's voice came suddenly, from out of the blue. And in a minute I was back Lord knows how many years back into the past, running in from the backyard of my childhood, my cricket bat banging on my knees. Her voice was hurrying me: 'Boy, we going to Deepaul house, come quick!'

I changed my shorts and pasted down my hair with coconut oil.

'And wash you hands, you can't walk in people deadhouse like that!'

Up Deepaul them front-step with that mad dog of theirs howling and pulling at his chain. Someone shouted, *how come the dog didn't take the death?*

Myself and Nasmeen Deepaul sat down on the front veranda drinking sorrel, watching the coming and going and the crying, snippets of conversation jumping out from inside the house –

'…that what you expect when you don't put nothing by … you never know when the Lord see fit to call you … awee gon punish now, punish!'

The next day Mother hired Govin's donkey cart and had taken us down to town, threatening me not to say a word to my father. I walked behind her into the Canada Bank, awed at the quiet atmosphere of order and efficiency: the bank clerks in shirt and tie, the women with short haircuts, swinging skirts and high heels clicking as they worked behind the counter or strode to open cabinets or disappeared through a door marked 'Private'. When it was our turn, we sat in a panelled room, whose walls were covered with paintings and certificates. Then I understood, I was there with my knowledge of reading and writing to help Mother open a savings plan for me! I never forgot that, you know, that sense of importance, my signature beside the mark of a mother who couldn't read or write, at the birth as it were, of the very means which would pay my airfare and start me off in London; this represented the planting of a seed, the power to control one's life. This sensible approach never left me, and I would return to it time and again whenever madness wanted to overtake me.

My boss came in then, and we had a conversation about Joycelyn, a very English conversation…

'Ah Eliot, you're in. Had a good weekend? How's Joycelyn?'

'Fine, fine, thank you Euan, And you?'

'Quite well, had that stroke of golf yesterday after lunch. Shame you couldn't make it over.'

'Well, Joycelyn isn't really up to it at the moment, you know…'

'Yes, yes, of course, of course … what's the latest?'

'She has to go for more tests next week.'

'You know you only have to say if you'd like any time off or anything…?'

'Thank you, Euan, but it's best I carry on, keep busy. Jocelyn certainly doesn't want me under her feet all the time.'

'Well, if you're sure. Pop into my office when you're ready, I'd like to go through those new accounts. Blasted interest rates have all got to be revised now. Those girls not in yet? It's damned well nine o'clock already. I expect we'll be making our own coffee next!'

Joycelyn was ill, you see, very ill. I don't know what it was set me off down memory lane that morning, but things just kept coming back to me all day. Before I knew it, my mind took me back to an old girl-friend called Maureen, must have been in the early seventies...

Maureen was from Trinidad. I had acquired a little room by then and I bumped into her as I got off the bus after work. My usual Friday night used to consist of two halves in the Red Lion followed by a fish and chip supper. Maureen had knocked back three rum and cokes to my half and puffed Marlborough smoke rings like a steam train around the red-leather-backed cubicle. There was an Irish vocalist I remember, a Matt Monro impressionist.

Maureen was saying my white skin should make things easy for me, 'You know, one o' my patients them does scream when she see is my black hands bringing she bed pan!'

I didn't have to tell Maureen about Mother, most of us in the Caribbean have mixed-blood, you know, that is how it is. But then I got to thinking about Roopnarine, and what shame I felt at what I had done, but whom do I blame, my Mother?

I was working in a factory at Vauxhall then, and one day one of the managers called me in.

'Right Eliot mate, come in my man, come in.'

He sat back, rocking on his chair, hands clasped behind his head.

'I thought you might be the chap to see, being from that part of the world and all. We've had an application for the junior clerk job, only thing, the young chap's black. Not that I'm racial, everybody knows me to be a liberal type, but I have to think of the others you see, harmonious atmosphere and all that. Besides, you employ one and before you know it, the shop floor's full of them. One of the boys was only saying the other day how multicultural his street was getting. But I'm prepared to give him a chance. Have a chat for me, see if you think he'll fit in.'

Strictly speaking, Roopnarine wasn't black, he was of Indian descent, but that's how things were going now, you see.

What the factory manager didn't know was that Roopnarine and me had history, that Roopnarine and me come from the very same village, and it was playing English cricket that had caused us to fall out when we were boys!

That year the West Indies cricket team had licked the England team bad-bad, as we would say! Every Guyanese schoolboy marked the pitch with renewed fervour, blessing the ball with spit and dust, playing and replaying the victory. I might not look it now, but I was a fast bowler when I was a boy! And Roopie didn't like that at all! Jealousy got him vex! He pushed me to the ground and beat me up well and proper, but is the things he said cause the trouble…

'Whitey shitey! You think this country still belang to you? What you know about cricket! I gun whup you ass fuh true!'

Roopnarine was calling me, who was every inch a Guyanese like him, the insult reserved for white people!

Mother put Mercurochrome on my cut forehead and sent me to bed early for fighting. But I couldn't sleep. I heard my father come back from the club, heard them talking long into the night.

'This is something we always expected, Janice. You can't live in a country like this and get off lightly. You know memories are long.'

Mother banged a plate on the table saying she didn't know how Pa could expect so little out of life and just because England wasn't good enough for him anymore didn't mean his son shouldn't have a chance. I heard Pa suck his teeth and ask, is that why you married me?

Now, these years later, there was Roopnarine smiling in front of me. He still had that way of standing almost on tiptoes, with his chest pulled right up. I guess it had something to do with his lack of height. How many times had I watched those shoulders bend, those short arms flexing his muscles before his heels lifted off with the dust of immortality? Our rivalry might have fizzled out when Roopnarine dropped out of school, turning his back on his family's cane-field work, and headed for Georgetown. But for me the cut branded white into my memory. Pa was right, memories were long.

There in the factory manager's side office I am ashamed to say I took Roopnarine's hand boldly, and after the surprise and greetings and 'How come you reach England man!' were over, I warned him off conspiratorially, how he would have a really bad time here man, spit in the tea that kind of thing, nothing noticeable that the discrimination people could jump on, you know what I mean man Roopnarine? Even I, Eliot, had to watch my back all the time!

Mother would have been proud of me. I'd worked bloody hard to get where I was. No matter how white I looked, how good an education I had, nothing had prepared me for the isolation, the sense of having to pull one's self up by the fingernails. I'd be damned if anybody was going to take it away from me!

'That boy's got possibilities,' my headmaster told Pa, 'good at cricket too. Could get a few of those if he put his mind to it,' he added, pointing to his Boston certificates.

Pa promised to have a word with me, and true to his word, he took me to the club and bought me a Banks beer.

'Your mother's got hopes for you, Eliot, expectations. She wants you in England, says there's nothing here for you. But England's no El Dorado my boy, not in any sense of the word. If it was up to me you'd stay right here where you belonged and make something of yourself. This country's crying out for good leaders. There's not much wrong with this life, at least a man has got respect.' He raised his hand then and beckoned the steward over.

With all the memories, I had quite forgotten about the letter. It wasn't until I phoned Joycelyn at lunchtime that I remembered.

'Everything okay?' I asked her.

One of the girls placed a sandwich and a cup of coffee in front of me.

'Letter? What letter? No I forgot all about it … all right I'll see you later.'

I slipped it out of my briefcase and stared at it. But the memories weren't ready to let go of me yet. Maureen popped back in my head. You young people may see an old man in front of you, you have to use your imagination and think of me as dashing back then in the seventies! They used to say I looked like Errol Flynn, and I wore a moustache like his. Us Caribbeans are dapper dressers too, or used to be!

'Eliot stop fretting. The woman deaf and anyway is my rent money keeping her in drink!', Maureen was saying.

I climbed the stairs after Maureen, my dress shoes swinging from my fingers. I don't know what possessed me to take her up on her offer. Women always seemed to be doing what they wanted with me. I remember thinking, I shouldn't have had that last drink! I could never hold my rum. Watching Pa pass out time and again in the yard had made me promise myself I'd raise my spirits at less cost to my own body.

Maureen was a new kind of woman then; none of that looking down at the ground and giggling like they didn't know what was on a man's mind. This new kind of woman was aeons away from the prototypes Pastor would chastise our congregation about back in Guyana, his angry tongue wagging, his eyes on the straight backs of the women in his pews, their wedding fingers encased in white gloves. The few years Maureen had been here, she confessed to me, had done more to wake her up to this jackass world than twenty years of child-bearing, child-raising, and woman-beating her God-fearing mother had endured. Under the ministrations of a woman who could drink, talk and smoke at the same time, I allowed myself a grudging respect for a woman's liberation that had made women so much more sexually available! Maureen was fun, and we parted friends, but I was looking for something else, someone who could replace the memory of innocence wrapped up in a church dress. I needed someone like Joycelyn, because all the time part of me held on to someone whose memory had never left me, someone who's name was Desiree.

Why now? I thought, looking at the letter. Why did it all have to come back and haunt me now that I had more or less smothered that whole grey mass of childhood? All those shadows, ghosts of dead ancestors. Pa on the front porch slapping mosquitoes, Mother in her church dress, her place in society raised by her marriage to an expatriate Englishman. My passion for Maureen had plugged the unfinished opening of my sexuality which had almost cost me my future. Desiree…

Where would I have been if it wasn't for Joycelyn? Her entrance into my life had been like a fresh breeze, uncluttered, untouched, unencumbered by baggage. She even wore yellow on our first date. She introduced me to a mother country I had been brought up to believe in, an England where one had tea in china, where the South Downs were gentle and sloping, where neatly clipped hedges and pleasantries over the garden fence established you, where Sunday Mass was bearable precisely because there was none of that hand-clapping *Hallelujah* nonsense. The move to the outskirts of Canterbury offered me an England far removed from the rootlessness of my first harsh years in England, where friendships never proceeded beyond a working life, where sometimes I had envied those close-knit communities to which my former boss at the factory had laughingly referred. Joycelyn's family, although scattered around the country, still came together at Christmas and summer parties, conversation skimming around local Council policy, the fox-hunting issue, the buying up of arable land. They welcomed me, I belonged. The recent purchase of the nearby oast, previously home to house-martins, owls, foxes and bats, had inspired countless debates between retaining of such landmarks to their original use or for souped-up modern buildings all glass and stone. I had a voice, I was an Englishman.

Mother spun round on her heels in the kitchen. I could hear the floor squeak and her gold bangles jangle.

'Eliot! Eliot! Is this what I raise you for, to marry some *dougla* woman?'

Memory took me away again, back to that little house by the cane-field. Desiree. Her skin gleaming bronze and copper, hair black as midnight, its rippling waves as gentle as the nearby creek. She had cried out like a sakiwinki and I had covered her mouth with my kisses; forgive me, relaying these intimate details to you. I never saw the baby, our baby. My mother later persuaded me that that night had never happened. Pointed to Pa slumped in the hammock, warning me that the time for white people's rule in Guyana was over and that I would have no place in it. Can I blame her now? The journey my mother had taken is the stuff of novels.

I knew that hand-writing. How many similar letters had Mother snatched away from the post-boy in the weeks leading up to my departure? Those hazy weeks that had swum and spun with visits to our Capital City, Georgetown; to Bookers for the suit, and the long hours waiting at the Embassy and the passport office. The goodbyes to this body and that body, strangers belonging to Mother from Black Bush Polder to Golden Grove … and Desiree's pinched face at the stelling, pressing against the crowd, her belly big with the baby I wasn't to know and the river swimming in a heat haze between us.

I slit open the envelope. No letter. A photograph: like her mother, but lighter, her eyes, even through my blurred vision, cool and grey. And a calling card: a lawyer now, and the new owner of the oast house.

Joycelyn was very ill, and I had to spare her the upset. She died a few months later. By the time I contacted my daughter she had already decided to leave. She had never forgiven me for leaving her mother anyway. Sold up, flew out to British Columbia where she said the planning regulations were more geared up to people with ambition, not a small-ass island whose glory days had come and gone.

I Tell You, the Taxi Driver Says

I can tell you more bleeding stories than you've had hot dinners. I've seen some sights and all, I tell you! You come far? Oh everybody round here is from somewhere else. Nobody stays the same place anymore. Take me now. Been driving cabs all me life, all me bleeding life. One time I thought I'd try my hand at something else, all kicked off I tell you. Been abroad though, oh yeah, me and my mate went walkabout before we settled down, this gap-year thing is nothing new I tell you. Times I pick students up, full of themselves like they're just discovering the world's just happened, you know what I mean? Full of themselves, I tell you. Take this geezer I pick up the other day. Don't ask me what he studied, it's all shit to me. But he was that excited he sat forward the whole time, not that I care if he wears his bleeding seat belt or not. But *I'm doing South America,* he tells me, *do you know Galapagos is being ruined?* No, I tells him, but what you going to do about it? Ruined? I can tell you about being ruined. This bleeding city's been ruined! They knock everything down then put it up again, causing more bleeding traffic jams than before. And the poor taxi driver … don't let me get started on that one! The thing is, what I tell everyone is, nothing's like we expect it is it? You know what I'm saying? Every bleeding blighter I pick up has a moan. Whether it's some poor woman jumping in by Wilkinson, or some American doo-dah coming down to earth off the Highspeed – it's all the bleeding same. *Fookin' ell,* she sez, *fookin' ell if I wasn't waiting in that bleeding queue at Tesco's and then they decide to open another one. And the time I decide to use the basket the bleeding bitch is counting how I've got more than 10 items in and don't do it again, as if I was a bleeding kid, the cocky bitch!* And don't start me off about Americans. Now you see me? I couldn't do this job if I could spill half the beans I got jumping round my plate. But sometimes you have to bite your lip, I tell you, when bleeding foreigners come in here full of shit about what England is. *Of course, you guys are hybrids,* this geezer sez, *with Roman, Danish and French blood* … well you tell me, you tell me, you think I can jump in a yellow cab in New York and say to some Chicano driver, *well of course you guys are all hybrids…!* He'll beat sheer shit outa me, or drop me off on some corner where the heavies will do me in pronto. That's the thing with the English, other people think they know more about us than we do!

That'll be a tenner mate.

Doing it Like Jamie Oliver

The person who shifted the axis on which Mr Wo's universe was settled was none other than his daughter Luisa. She had just turned thirteen the year Jamie Oliver was causing trouble up and down the country, intent on children eating healthy meals and on teachers implementing them. Mr Wo and his wife Theresa Lily watched in horror as badly-dressed, overweight parents marched up to school playgrounds and thrust bags of chips through the school-fence to armfuls of starving, waiting children.

'What is this country coming to! My God!'

Not Luisa though. Luisa came in chomping a McDonalds and said this was a free country and people should eat what they liked. There also appeared to be a certain slur to her voice, which was puzzling.

Mr Wo identified Canterbury as home. He loved the old stone and timbers, the towering Cathedral, the glitzy shops and the quiet of mornings. He couldn't rightly say he loved the loud young people who came out at night just when the tourists were going home. Mr Wo's business meant he had dealings with all kinds of people. Opening until midnight encouraged a friendly if businesslike approach. Mr Wo was very good at measuring the happiness of those who stumbled inebriated or irritable into his establishment. In fact he had a happiness cat on the counter, and was interested in how often customers would stroke it and say hey kitty kitty depending on how drunk they were. What he was not prepared to accept was that his daughter would be one of those.

Mr Wo's parents had left Hong Kong with a few thousand yuan and Hong Kong dollars sewed into the soles of their shoes and did what so many other immigrant people did: work, work, save, save, build, build. He remembered quite clearly a small backstreet shop in the Midlands, followed by another in Cardiff, then at last, happily, this present establishment, which his parents had bequeathed him. Marriage to Theresa Lily, the daughter of his father's old friend from Szechwan region allowed him to live and work contentedly as front of house, whilst Theresa Lily sliced, chopped, ground, whipped, sautéed, fried, steamed and banged saucepans.

Mr Wo often thought about the preconceptions of what was thought of as Chinese. Noodles, black beans, and soy sauce. Opium dens and sailors. Kung fu movies, triads and backgammon. Actually, that was quite a lot. But he did wonder what people would think if they knew how much he liked Country and Western. Apart from these perceived concerns, Mr Wo rarely encountered racism of the type that could be so prevalent. Although history would inform you of many unjust attacks on the Chinese race in Victorian England, including even riots in Cardiff in nineteen hundred and something, his people had come into their own now. There might be Chinese restaurants from Merthyr Tydfil to Glasgow, and you could argue the authenticity of Chinese cooking until the parrot danced, but Chinese people were also businessmen and entre-preneurs, they were TV fashionistas and scientists. Look at that Gok Wan and that little Susie on The Apprentice TV show! Chinese people had so much to be proud of! Mr Wo had also recently watched a programme on how China was transforming the continent of Africa. A small part of Mr Wo thought he might have been more than a take-away restaurant owner.

In Mr Wo's restaurant, China was represented by a gold and scarlet calendar sent out each year by the Hong Kong Abroad Business Consortium, an organisation that worked hard to maintain links with the home country. This hung on the wall above the counter, and bore the full force of any gusts of wind or cold drafts of air that entered with a customer, and by the end of the year, the pages were furled and tired, just in time for the arrival of a new one. This calendar was one of many small things that had begun to irritate his daughter, including the miniature pa-goda made out of bamboo sticks and even the name that had been painstakingly hand-painted ten years ago, The Golden Dragon.

'For Christ's sake, Dad,' she had stormed, 'isn't it about time you updated this place?'

Mr Wo was not an intolerant man. He knew you had to keep in step with a changing society. He had made one very important improvement: a new glass-topped coun-ter. He had gone to great lengths to get this right; had abandoned the paper menus that had hung limply (like the calendar in November) on a plastic stand on the coun-ter, the costs of which had escalated. He knew that each customer who had slipped one in their handbag or pocket was sentencing his beautiful artwork to the paper pile by the microwave or the coffee table, gathering dust on mantelpieces, jostling alongside others from the opposition: Kebab House Special, Pizza for You, Thai Cuisine. Over the years these scoundrels had moved in on a market once exclusively the right of the Indian and Chinese, going so far as to send their staff to post their colourful leaflets through letter-boxes from Sturry to Ashford. Mr Wo had never contemplated doing that, not once. Theresa Lily had raised the subject once, after a particularly doleful trip to the supermarket to research the escalation of choice for Chinese ready meals at greatly reduced prices than The Golden Dragon could offer. But Mr Wo had put his size six feet down firmly insisting that the provision of quality fresh food, together with their so far untarnished reputation, meant they did not have to sink to such depths. Indeed he had inscribed that as a sub-text in the newly re-designed and re-positioned menu that lay attractively beneath his new glass-topped counter and online, oh yes online. Let them walk uphill and down dale, he had told Theresa Lily, and indicated recycling bags on the street full of such dispersible litter. Most people coming for a take-away knew what they were coming for anyway; top of the list was chicken chow-mein, prawn fried rice, and barbequed spare ribs.

Interest in Chinese food had waxed and waned over the years, persuaded by season, economics, changing eating patterns, and a myriad of others as is the case with all things. Mr Wo could trace the history of Chinese food in the UK in one sentence: Vesta, Ken Hom, woks, Asda and Beijing. But they were still surviving, even with the emergence of fly-by-night eateries such as Aussie Billabong and Trinidadian Souse Sistuhs. Did they last? No way José. Not like The Golden Dragon, as constant and timeless as The Cathedral.

In 2000 Mr Wo and Theresa Lily made the trip to end

all trips to mainland China and Hong Kong. For both of them it was a homecoming, both spiritual and emotional. As well as visiting the Great Wall, the Yangtze, and the Terracotta Warriors, they revisited ancestral sites and met with old and young far-reaching members of the family. Luisa was a small sweet child then, a delicious eight-year-old who was embraced, tickled and indulged a million times. They all tried to restrain themselves with the customary acceptable behaviour, but left with hearts that were both empty and full at the same time; Mr Wo coming away with numbness in his fingers from the tight grip his old aunt, a sister of his mother's, inflicted on saying goodbye. Theresa Lily returned with traditional recipes entered into the notepad of her mobile and small packets of dried condiments, whose natures ranged from fifty-year-old eggs to dried seahorses, inserted into secret pockets of her luggage.

The one thing you could not say about Mr Wo was that he did not take life's lessons on board. Indeed Mr Wo's whole life was one of adapting to each toss of the ball that life threw him. There had been an English girl he would have liked to have gone out with, and some guys with whom he would have liked to have gone on a gap-year. But he yielded to his parents' commitment to business and put these fickle dreams aside. He had not been unhappy. His Theresa was every bit as saucy as a wife should be, and it wasn't her fault they had only had one child, a daughter. Mr Wo thought of the trouble he might have had with sons. His friend Roger in Birmingham had such wild boys, mixing drugs and rap music. His eye would always water with joy when he remembered the first day they brought Luisa home, the dark, knowing eyes and shock of black hair; and so many milestones – her first birthday, her first day at nursery, her school photos, and her certificates for piano.

Mr Wo would not agree that Luisa was spoilt. Would not agree that perhaps he had over-indulged her in ways his parents had not, due to either circumstance or desire, indulged him. Therefore he had not limited his daughter's social life. From the beginning she had gone to as many parties as she had been invited to, apart from that one from the child of the loud-mouthed mother who fell through the doors of The Golden Dragon quite frequently. He had driven her himself to fancy-dress and Tinkerbell parties, to Harry Potter and McDonalds parties, to swimming parties and parties where parents hired clowns and magicians, and even at the age of nine, a stretch limo party. He had driven her to ballet and music classes, to karate and piano. He had allowed her sleepovers and a mobile phone from the age of ten, and stayed out of all matters regarding decoration of her room, a task he left quite happily to Theresa Lily. He had also made it a point that he knew, if not all her friends, at least he had met their parents and knew where they lived. This had become more difficult of late of course, due to the secretive natures of teenagers.

It is to be said that it was through Luisa's school and social life, like so many parents who move or migrate from one place to another, that Mr Wo and Theresa made friends here. And Mr Wo hoped there had come a moment when they had stopped being seen as the Chinese restaurant people to become Timmy and Theresa, Luisa Wo's parents. So when eventually at school plays and dance rehearsals some of the parents waved, 'Oh hi, Tim!' in the gaggle of the dressing-room, Mr Wo, already a happy man, became happier still. Now they had a good circle of friends, whose barbeques were always enriched with Theresa's special chicken in barbeque sauce. Integration was the key, he and his wife both agreed, and Mr Wo was quite happy for Theresa to go to pilates on a Monday night whilst he put his feet up and listened to his beloved Country and Western.

Now Mr Wo and Theresa Lily turned to look at their daughter and for the first time realised that they were looking at a young person whose accent carried inflections of outer London, urban Jamaican and Australian. That neither had noticed this before was slightly worrying, but then most parents have this kind of surprising revelation at some time during their child's teenage years. But worse than this, was the fact it appeared their daughter had been drinking.

Mr Wo, disturbed by what he saw as a worrying indication of what had the potential to become A Problem in the Family, decided instantly that Luisa's ultimate transformation into a worthy member of society was now on his shoulders and the slightly smaller shoulders of his wife.

A programme for the transformation of Luisa's propensity for unacceptable behaviour was, over the next few days, drawn up. From now on Luisa's social activities would be greatly reduced and she would spend more time studying, this with the aid of a home tutor whose number Mr Wo obtained from his social network of parents. Having cast a critical eye over Luisa's last school report, Mr Wo realised that it was actually not very good. Why had he not noticed this before? He remembered Luisa quickly pointing out her excellent marks for Citizenship and Drama, and being distracted from looking closely at the others as she proceeded to play him Beyoncé's new song on the piano. Now, looking at it closely, he could see that Maths and English was almost borderline! This from a daughter who had always got good marks. This was not good, not good at all. He had never intended to be a heavy father, or lay the future of the restaurant at his daughter's feet. She could do as she wished once she had finished her education. He did have secret dreams of her becoming a pianist, of course, but would not have contemplated putting his daughter through that *Britain's Got Talent* nonsense. But whether Luisa wanted to act, or become an engineer, she still needed her education!

So what to do? He asked Theresa Lily to cast an eye over Luisa's wardrobe to make sure she wasn't slipping out of the house wearing clothes that were too short or too tight. He knew full well this request might be futile, that girls went to their friends' houses and changed there. Mr Wo was not a prude, but this was his daughter they were talking about, god damn.

He drew up a chart of treats to be dished out when Luisa did as expected, sensible treats like being allowed to go to the cinema with friends, or having friends over. He also drew up a list of what he was loath to describe as punishments, but rather described them as 'helping character to form'. These included the withdrawal of pocket money, confiscation of mobile phone, or of any treat that had already been agreed.

Theresa did not agree with all of these. Since she had been going to pilates she had been looking leaner, had altered her hairstyle, and had become argumentative. Mr Wo hoped that he wouldn't have to be fighting a battle on two fronts. His wife insisted that a reward earned must not be taken away.

Over the next six months the rooms behind The Golden Dragon became a battleground. Saucepans were banged loudly and frequently. Bedroom doors were slammed with the power of a force 9 gale. Mr Wo's happiness cat lost her head during one of these. Outwardly the Wos appeared gracious and pleasant as usual, although it was remarked on that Theresa's special Chinese barbeque chicken was very much missed, even though the new Jamie Oliver version was delicious.

Although Luisa argued and stropped about all the new restrictions, and went so far as to threaten to call Childline, she did, after six months or so, grudgingly apply herself to her studies. She ended her relationship with her piano, whether because she knew this would hurt her father deeply, or she simply lost interest, only she knew.

But Mr Wo knew she was like a bird in a cage, just like those they had seen in the markets of Hong Kong, songbirds, field birds, nightingales, birds from mainland China trapped in bamboo cages. Her dark eyes strayed beyond him to the open door.

His wife too, was changing, had joined zumba classes on a Thursday night, a decision that had seen the employment of a new chef, a cousin from Manchester who travelled down for the day and stayed overnight. Mr Wo tried not to think about the money. He couldn't understand either why Theresa had recently voiced a desire for glued-on eyelashes.

Now Mr Wo has taken to going for an evening walk each night after shutting the shop. He is tired of course, after standing on his feet for six hours taking orders and running back and forth to the kitchen, but has decided he needs the exercise. He is wondering whether he should introduce deliveries, which will mean extra staff.

He walks along Northgate, circles the Cathedral, and heads towards Dane John Gardens. Sometimes he walks along the city walls, and looks down at this city he has made his home. He hums some of his favourite Country and Western tunes, Merle Haggard, Dolly Parton or Johnny Cash. If no-one is around he might even sing some of the lyrics aloud; there is something about a dark starry night, empty of people, that invites such exhibitionism.

Mr Wo gets to thinking about China then, the little he has seen of it, the great Yangtze rushing through the mighty cliffs, the tight grip of his aunt's hands. These are the very same stars above China, he thinks, the very same stars. *Who of my people are watching these stars the same time as me?* He doesn't care what the time difference is, he just likes the thought.

He just wishes he knew why that song by Tammy Wynette, *D.I.V.O.R.C.E.*, keeps going round and round in his head.

The Migration of Goddesses

There's been that many goings on in here I've lost count. From mums and toddlers to the history lot, from coffee mornings to the choirs … they breeze in with their paraphernalia, share their moments of glory and indecision then breeze out again. Some are more fun than others, the carnival lot for instance, with their coloured paper and sticks and glue and papier-mâché giant women. One got stuck in the nave one year, took her head clean off.

There's weeklies and there's one-offs; this was a one-off. Kaya arrived, biting her lower lip and weighed down with a portfolio of posters.

Gord banged through the heavy doors.

'Hiya Kaya! Someone's working hard!'

She wiped her hands on the back of her jeans and called him over. 'Grab that hammer and help me with this will you?'

He came closer, peering at the poster she was attempting to fix on the display screen. 'Who's that?'

'The Black Madonna of course.'

'Oh. Is that, she … part of the display then?'

She shot him a look.

'Naturally.'

He walked along the stage, taking in the dozen or so images stapled to the screens.

Some of them he recognised: The Madonna holding the Baby, a many-armed blue Goddess from India, the Chinese Kwan Yin. The others he peered at closely, squinting his eyes. He stopped and pointed.

'What's this one?'

'Lilith, of course, you fool, Adam's wife.'

He frowned, 'Wasn't that Eve?'

She rolled her eyes.

'You know Gord, it's for people like you I'm doing this workshop. You've been that brainwashed you don't know shit.'

He pulled his shoulders up assertively.

'Well, you'd better not be speaking to people like that when they come – *if* they come. They'll all walk out on you.'

She shrugged. 'So? It's their loss then; "when the pupil is ready the teacher will appear".'

He laughed.

'You know, it's a good thing I'm your friend; you're such a smartass.'

She glared at him angrily.

'Gord*on* Bradley…'

'What are you two arguing about?'

Neither of them had heard the door go. Francine was walking across the floor of the church hall carrying a large wicker basket. She had one of those African shawls wrapped round her waist and across her back and shoulders. A tiny blond head nestled against her chest. Gord jumped down from the stage and hurried to help her. Together they lifted the basket up onto a table and Francine began to lift out tablecloths and paper plates, a warm aroma of fresh baking rising up as she opened up containers of home-made cakes, quiches, and sausage rolls.

'That smells heavenly!' Gord said, reaching out tentatively for a sausage roll. Francine slapped his hand sharply.

'Don't you dare!'

Kaya came to join them. She glanced at the baby briefly.

'You've been busy. There's an urn through there,' she indicated the kitchen, 'you all right with doing the teas?'

'Sure.' Francine indicated the display on the stage – 'That looks good. I'll have a look in a moment.' She rested her hand on top of the baby's head. 'Do you have any idea how many are coming?'

Kaya shrugged. 'Not really. My women's group are and some from the community centre. One or two from the uni have promised. But I don't want to preach to the initiated; I'm really hoping some new people will come. Plus I've got to fill in that stupid form for the funding.'

'I'm sure it'll be fine,' Francine smiled. 'Some of the mums from the baby group are coming. It's good having it this time of day.'

She looked at Gord. 'How about your lot, Gord; any of them?'

'Can't promise, they kind of think it's for women…'

'Well that's where they're wrong,' Kaya said sharply. 'This workshop is supposed to look at the feminine in all of us, and that includes men!'

'Yeah, I know, but you know how guys are…' He picked up one of the advertising leaflets: *Your Inner Feminine: Goddesses, the Modern Woman and Man's Herstory.*

'We discussed the wording of that,' Kaya said. 'Over and over.'

'Yeah I know,' he repeated, 'it's just really difficult isn't it? Putting the words "feminine" and "man" together … you know how limited guys' thinking is; well, just look at me,' he grinned.

'Well, if you're an example of what there is, it's best no-one else comes.'

A couple of his mates did turn up. Kaya wasn't to know that Gord had bribed them. He fancied Kaya like crazy even though his mates called her a ball breaker.

She could run a good workshop, you could give her that. Gord watched as she opened the workshop with a slideshow, depicting images of a string of Goddesses he'd never even heard of. He was surprised to learn that that Black Madonna person wasn't really black, not in the African sense like. Gord wondered where she had dug out all these fantasy women from. She moved from Greece to Rome, dropped in on India, where Gord was intrigued by that Kali chick. Right penis-crusher that one, terrifying! Then Kaya was talking about the ones she referred to as 'silent Bible women', a few Marys, the Magdalene, Ruth…

She spent a long time on the Magdalene. 'There are,' she paused dramatically, 'literally hundreds of images of this Mary.'

Gord tried to remember what he had learned in Sunday school; wasn't Mary Jesus' mother? Didn't she wash his feet too? He was confused.

Kaya had included several images of this Mary in the slideshow. 'From fallen creature to saint,' she said, pointing out the range of perceptions of the Magdalene. But… Here she paused again and looked meaningfully at her audience: '*Whose* image?'

Gord had noticed her doing a head-count before she

started and was pleased for her that there were one or two people she didn't know. Good, she had to prove there was a need for this workshop; if it was successful she could do the kind of thing she really wanted to do, a big affair with seminars and authors, controversial discussions between priestesses, priests and imams. Kaya was sick to death of how little people knew, and what they thought was ethnic and 'real'.

One of the guys chirped in,

'You mean, like, who was the artist?'

'Precisely.' Kaya gave one of her rare smiles.

She made a sweeping gesture at the images on display.

'All of these images are the perspective of the artists and the time they lived in; we need to remember that, when we look at any painting, representation is always tempered by the morals and restrictions of the time.' She paused; 'However, *however* … the representation of women in art is *particularly* contentious, politically fraught, condescending, and power-controlling…'

'Doesn't that go for men as well though?', one of Gord's mates chirped in.

'Some of the old paintings showed men in some bloody awful situations!'

'Yeah, like crucifixions! And battles!'

'But what do you think when you look at them?'

'They're idiots!'

Gord kicked his mate underneath the chair. Kaya's wrath wasn't worth the price of one pint, never mind two.

Kaya wasn't going to let the guys run the show. 'They are heroes, and martyrs! Remember, most of these artists were men, and the images we get from paintings of women are extremely polarised, Virgin or Whore.'

She pointed at what she called 'One of the more disturbing images of Mary Magdalene, portrayed as a temptress in a temple, surrounded by men literally looking down at her. How does this painting make you feel?'

Francine put her hand up tentatively.

'She does look a bit like a … prostitute?'

'Yes, that's quite clear,' said Kaya.

One of the women from the uni spoke up.

'But isn't that how she was depicted in the Bible? Until Jesus "saved" her, that is!'

'And wasn't she one of the women at the tomb?'

'We can see several perceptions of her right away!'

'So what's wrong with an artist painting an *aspect* of a woman? Surely it's not possible to present women in their multi-dimensional entirety?'

'Okay, let's look at it this way; generally speaking, how many of you think women have got a rough deal, in being presented negatively and one-dimensionally, and how much do you think Art is responsible for this?'

Kaya looked out into her audience. They were looking at her with engaged faces though some of the guys were looking quite cocky, as if they were as a group relishing the role of representational masters of women.

'I don't know much about Art,' this from one of the new women, 'but if the Daily Star is anything to go by, women are still all tits and bums!'

'They'd look a bit rubbish in their office suit, pen behind the ear in oils like!'

This caused a bit of a snigger amongst them all, apart from the uni crowd. One of the guys pointed out that women's magazines were just as bad, showing sexy blokes like that Matthew McConaughey with his shirt off.

The discussion wasn't quite going in the direction Kaya had planned, but she knew sometimes this happened, you couldn't control people. She needed to pull it back at this point though.

'I want to move on to talk about some of the many aspects of women as represented by the several Goddesses that are known of. It's good that we've related the subject to modern day women; in fact there's a perfect example of this that we can begin with – how many of you have heard Earl Spencer's speech that he made when his sister, Lady Diana, died? He likened his sister to the Goddess Diana, hounded by the press as the Goddess Diana herself was hunted by dogs. Coincidence or archetype? Some of you might be too young to remember, but wasn't Diana Spencer portrayed as virtuous, beautiful, charitable? Until she 'tarnished' her persona by hanging out with Dodi, that was. What do you think of the idea of this grisly end as being seen as some sort of punishment for the destruction of this saintly image? Do you think there was any universal retribution or just coincidence?'

'Coincidence of course,' one of the uni group said, 'she was hounded before she even met Dodi!'

'Oh, I don't know,' Francine said, 'it has got a kind of ring to it, you know, kind of like stepping on a path in life that you know is fraught with a particular danger…'

'Okay, it's all ingredients for reflection and analysis; we'll all really never know. What's important for this workshop is we see how myth and fact can blend to add layers of how men and women can and should behave, and how much of that we're responsible for. In the next session we're going to be looking at archetypes, what femininity means and the feminine that exists in us all. I'd just like to end this session by bringing your attention to the list of Goddesses and how they are aligned with certain characteristics such as 'The Lady of the Beasts', a goddess representative of nature in all its forms…'

The door banged open again. A young girl with a mangy-looking dog stood there.

Kaya beckoned her in.

'You're welcome,' she said, 'but you can't really bring the dog in. Can you leave it outside?'

The girl, a waif in ripped jeans and an Indian scarf round her head, held onto the chain tightly and shook her head. 'No she'll run away she will, she don't like having me outa her sight.'

Kaya sighed.

She looked round at the others. 'Anybody mind?'

They shrugged and shook their heads.

'Let's just hope the vicar doesn't come in.'

The waif sat down on one of the chairs in the circle. The dog sat too, her head alert, panting.

'I caught a bit of what you were saying; sounded dead interesting that.'

'Which bit, exactly?' asked Kaya.

'About women having bits of Goddesses in them like.'

Kaya nodded and looked down at her notes.

'We're really talking about archetypes, you know, a bit different from stereotypes.'

'Well Ise always liked animals,' the waif said, 'does it mean like I'm like that Lady of the Beasts you was on about?' She giggled nervously, and looked round at the group. 'I can grab the beasts bit, I was always bringing stray things 'ome. But I ain' no lady though!'

Kaya felt they were going off the strand – what she had been hoping to go on to discuss was the way that small-minded representation of women had gone on to do harm in men themselves, by denying the inner feminine in their consciousness. She just hoped things went more according to plan when they were involved in the activity.

They broke for refreshments after the slide show. Kaya chose this time to go round chatting to people, and try and break the ice a bit more. She'd got a fair crowd in the end, but some of the women from the mums and toddlers seemed unsure about what to say, as if they didn't want to sound stupid.

Afterwards they were given some exercise sheets and

put into pairs, the questions focusing on the difference between stereotypes and archetypes, with a list of Goddesses and their attributes to choose from. They were asked to tick all the characteristics that they recognised in themselves. Kaya had split Gord and his mates up, and paired them with women, although in some cases it was unevenly balanced. The guys sat back in their seats with their arms crossed. However, the nature of the workshop meant they had to take part in the end, paired with a partner who had to ask them questions. There was a hum around the room, maybe it was working after all. Kaya herself had sat with the waif, whose name turned out to be Kera, of all things. The girl was staring down hard at her sheet, concentrating.

'Well I ain' this one!' she said, after a few minutes. 'Demeter. Body as vessel. Earth mother. Def not me.'

'It doesn't mean you won't be at another time,' Kaya said.

'Ow? I ain' gonna change am I?'

'It's not that we change; it means that different aspects of the Goddesses are present in us at different times. Take me for instance, I definitely have aspects of Athena in me … look here.'

She drew a line with her fingernail down to Athena on the chart. 'Athena, Goddess of Civilisation. Intellectual, and logical. That just means I like studying and I'm practical! There may be a time though, perhaps if I become a mum, thought that's not on my agenda at the moment! But then I may exhibit aspects of these Goddesses here…'

'What about all them foreign Goddesses though?' Kera pointed at the African Yemanja. 'Surely that ain't got nothing to do wi' us? I seen they had a Mexican one in the last carnival, what's da' all about?'

'If you look closely you'll see that all Goddesses from all over the world inhabit universal attributes; they are simply localised according to where they originate. A tribe living next to a river therefore will naturally worship water. What's interesting is how the male and female get to represent different things, like iron, for war, or fruit, for fertility. Unfortunately although women represent potentially powerful features of the world, they are still subjugated in real life. Look at how some cultures call their country a 'motherland' and yet their real women are treated appallingly! As for the importing of Goddesses into our culture, some travel with people as they migrate, but also unfortunately are 'borrowed' if they're seen as 'cool' for the moment!'

'Yeah,' Kera said, nodding. 'Well, I'm well thirsty, you talking about water; any chance of another cuppa tea?'

Lunch brought a minor calamity: Kera's dog, nostrils tantalised by the aroma of Francine's baking, leapt onto the table flinging sausage rolls and paper plates into the air and wolfing down as much as she could before Kera and Gord managed to grab hold of her. The women screamed as she gave her captors the slip, and watched in horror as she bounded round the church hall, leaping on chairs and across the stage, skidding past Kaya's displays. She paused there, against a backdrop of a dozen portraits of Goddesses from all across the world, enjoying her momentary freedom, her tail wagging, just giving Kera time to slip her lead back on.

'I'm really sorry, 'she said, 'she must be well 'ungry, she don't usually behave like that.'

'You'll have to leave,' Kaya said sharply, 'people could have been hurt here.' She turned to face the others, 'I'm sorry about this everyone, are you all okay?'

Some of them nodded slowly, one or two were muttering.

'I shoulda known we would'na been welcome 'ere,'

Kera was saying huffily, 'this being a church and all, I thought we'd be welcome. Ain't no fun living on the streets y'know.'

'Well I'm sorry if that's the only reason you came in here,' Kaya said coldly, 'I thought you were interested in the workshop.'

Kera sniffed. 'Tell you what I do know, Miss Fancy Pants; I know my Bible and I know that Jesus welcomed everyone, that Magdalene Mary, robbers and thieves! If he was 'ere now it'd be people like me'd be in his gang, I betcha!'

Kaya looked at her astounded. For once she was lost for words.

The upheaval certainly shifted the tone of the workshop. On Kera's departure, the group assembled once again, to feedback their sessions on archetypes. The guys had taken part unwillingly, and refused to see any significance in their personality traits that might have been influenced by how women were or are represented. Francine's baby, frightened by the dog, cried throughout the rest of the session. The uni women were interested in the academic study of what they called Jungian interpretations of spirituality, whilst a couple of the new women said they weren't sure if they'd done it right and one of them had a friend who was a Buddhist and another was learning to play bhangra drums. Kaya was sure she overheard someone saying something about missing tai chi as she handed them all a feedback form.

It was while she was clearing up that she thought to glance up at the stained-glass window above the porch. For some reason shreds of coloured tissue hung like bunting from raised rivets of lead. She didn't know what they were of course. I could have told her it was the ribbons from the

Mexican Giant Goddess' head, trapped there since last summer. But her mind, fractured already by the unexpected frissons of the workshop, grew feathers and beads, whispered to her parables she barely remembered from Sunday School behind which stood small stories of real women: Martha begrudging her role; Lot's wife looking back.

The feedback forms fluttered to the floor, and Gord, on his way back from paying off his mates in the porch, helped her clear up, thinking what a tough little thing she was really, with her head up high like that.

On the Road to Canterbury

So we clambered out of Gaz's car like escaped canaries. It was Sav, Rafe, Gaz, me and a sweet-looking guy called Biz, all students from the uni.

It felt like a road trip as we exited the city, which was dead on a Sunday anyway, and headed for Grove Ferry. The sun was shinin', the music was playin'; what more could a girl ask?

Gaz pulled into the car park just missing kids and dogs and shouting mums. All heading for their roast dinners and piss-ups and watching the boats bobbing on the water. Yeah, right, get a life.

None of us had enough money for drinks, but Gaz had a half-ounce of Moroccan and a bottle of Scotch, and after shaking our heads in disgust at the pastoral riverside scene we headed for the hills, clambering like goats across the railway line and up the embankment. Gaz lived here so he knew what's what. We crawled over and under barbed wire and tumbled into a field full of sheep shit.

But higher up, the grass was soft and clean and there was an oak tree to lean on and lie under as we passed round the Scotch and what seemed to be a never-ending circle of joints. Sav was saying her dad would kill her if he knew what she was up to and send her straight back to Mumbai. We just laughed, thinking it hysterically funny, promising to tie the wheels of the aeroplane to Gaz's motor and doing sit-ins at Heathrow. We could spread dissent through Facebook and throw a cordon around the plane. Rafe had brought his guitar and was just getting ready to play something when Biz farted and the sheep by the fence started running and we all fell about laughing and Biz rolled down the hill and fell in the patch with the sheep shit.

The afternoon stretched as interminably as the never-ending roll-past of puffballs of cloud. Sam and Rafe disappeared for a while and their giggles were lost behind a gorse hedge. Gaz's eyes were bluer than the sky, and was going on and on about Mill and his ideas on liberty and how the man was talking bollocks man, there was no such thing as liberty, every breath we took was pre-ordained and programmed and Biz said he needed a shit for real and did anyone have any tissues?

Tomorrow's deadline was looming in my mind which I decided was smaller than Gaz's. Why the fuck was I reading that boring crap *Villette* when all I really wanted to do was go round the world in a campervan? I rolled over onto my stomach and saw the spire of the Cathedral settled in comfortably between gently sloping hills.

Someone must have said the words 'time' and 'go' and in a haze we scrambled back over the barbed wire, not without injury, but of course we didn't feel it, and rolled down the embankment screaming *Timber!* and *Bear Hunt!*

We re-entered the family gatherings grass-stained and

sheep-stained, yodelling and whooping like the warriors we'd become. We managed to pool enough money between us for ice-creams without the 99 and the cold sweet taste was soothing to a tongue smoky and raw.

We were driving back through the city when I felt it. The lurch in my stomach, the acid in my mouth. The others were laughing at something or other and from far away I heard a voice I remembered from childhood, 'I think I'm going to be sick'.

Gaz wheeled round the roundabout by the bus station and did an emergency stop. I pushed the door open and spilt my guts out just outside the city walls.

Shop till you

drop you bitches

Natasha stood sullenly inside the wide screen of glass and looked at her watch. 4.15. Another forty-five minutes of standing in her boring role as greeter, *Hello, how are you today?* as a steady stream of what she called losers rippled through the doorway. She hated when it was her turn to be a greeter. Hated being the dummy that spoke, that sometimes frightened the customers when she moved, hated parting her perfect lips and showing her crooked teeth.

There's nothing the matter with your teeth, her stupid mother told her. *And if there was it's only your own bleeding fault for not letting the dentist fix braces when he said.*

Natasha was happy with most other parts of her body. Liked being tall and slim, liked inheriting her mother's golden skin and green eyes, liked standing out wherever she strolled, walked in, went clubbing, whatever. If it wasn't for her blinking teeth she could have been a model, she was sure of it.

Hello, how are you today?

The baby in the pushchair scowled at her and threw his dummy on the floor. His slag mother didn't even notice, too busy shoving her tattooed arm through the rack of summer frocks. Natasha had no intention of picking it up; she saw what these mums did, sucked the dirt off and handed it back to their sickly-looking children.

Natasha wasn't having a good day; she was feeling guilty.

Back in her locker the wallet lay hidden in her handbag. She could sense its presence through the walls that separated them. It was like a heart beating in slow motion; she could see it pulsating even though what she was actually looking at was Canterbury shopping precinct with its Saturday afternoon carnivalesque cast of characters. Maybe it wasn't the wallet, maybe it was those arty-farty tossers out there who'd been banging away on those big wooden drums with their stilt-walker friends and their dangly things on sticks. Natasha didn't know what it was all about and she didn't care. It was bad enough having to put up with her mother and whatsisname having weirdo people round with guitars and didgeridoos, so that when *her* mates came round Natasha felt they were the teenagers, not her, and would head straightaway upstairs to her room and drown them all out with a slam of the door and headphones.

4.30

There was four hundred quid in there. Who the fuck carried cash like that around? They deserve to lose it, tossers. Think of what she could do with that money. She could go to Ibiza for the roadshow with Lizzie and co. She could go to the V Festival. She could buy an entire new wardrobe. She could see an orthodontist.

It wasn't even as if she had been looking for anything. There'd been no karmic warning, no feeling as she got out her bed that morning that she'd be in for anything out of the ordinary. There she was, minding her own business, dragging her dedicated self down her own road at eight-thirty in the morning and there it was, wedged between the pavement and an old wrought-iron fence. She'd stubbed her toe first on one of those manky cobblestones some plonker thought were Olde English and cool but no-one could walk on, and she'd looked down and there it was. Knew it immediately, somebody's wallet, some bloke's maybe, as it had no photos or nothing, just the money and a scratchcard. She'd opened it of course, who wouldn't? And the twenties just leapt out at her, and straightaway she'd shoved it in her bag. Now it lay waiting in her locker in the stockroom beating with a steady pulsating rhythm that was giving her a bloody headache.

Hiya, Tash, you all rite?

There was Lizzie, all smiles and new jeans, fresh from Next. She didn't have to bloody work for a living, off to uni to study something absurd.

Wotcha, Liz, yeah im alrite, just pissed off you know. She lowered her voice, she needed the job and you never knew who was standing behind the Sale Rail.

You going out tonight?

Might do, who else is out?

Victoria's having a barbi first with the parents I think she and Collette are coming out.

Wicked. Yeah I'm up ferrit, whatever.

Brill, text me lata.

Who wanted to go to uni anyway? Fat lot of good it had

done her mother; still ended up working as a glorified maid.

Only the other day Natasha had been reading about all those graduates out of work, and all the money they owed. Look at her now, straight out of school and always managed to get some job, crap though most of them were. It wasn't as though she was stupid or nothing, just wasn't interested. But she was fed up with people always asking her what she wanted to do. What the fuck did it matter? Who at 19 knows what they want to spend the rest of their life doing? It wasn't as if there was that much choice anyway. Screw your head up studying, wear your feet down working, or get pregnant and have the choice made for you. Most of her mates didn't know what they wanted to do, except for those who had money and back-packed from Thailand to Peru.

The stilt-walker was packing up. Thank Christ for that. Lunatic. Let him take his mate and his poxy drums as well. What has all that got to do with the real world? Christ, you only had to look at their clothes to know they were weirdos. Natasha looked down at her ballet pumps, good for standing, and the rows of summer clothes around her, some hanging drunkenly off their hangers with all the handling they'd had all day. Guess who was going to have to straighten them all up before she went home. At least the shop-floor was thinning out now. She sighed. Thank Christ, she could stop greeting. She could now stand nearer to the door, hand on the lock and wish them all goodbye with all the real pleasure in the world. Most of them just spent their time spending other people's money with no care in the world.

First day off she had, that's what she was going to do. Sod conscience. Whoever dropped it must've been a loser. She deffo wasn't one. Finders keepers.

Sugar Water

He saw her again tonight. Running ahead in the rain, through the darkened streets, like that figure in the film, *Don't Look Now.*

You couldn't mistake Canterbury for Venice, no matter how much it rained. Nor, for that matter, could you mistake it for Guyana. But the narrow streets at night, especially those with cobbles, with old houses leaning like whisperers, weaving outwards from the Cathedral and the lines of ever-increasing modernised shops, teased you into seeing canals and washing hanging like faded flags in the yellow light.

His grandmother Desdemona.

He'd always been told, as a boy and afraid of jumbies, that water stops ghosts travelling, so, *move on boy, go abroad*. And you couldn't get drier than this city. Canterbury's Stour was but a shallow stream now, and the boatman's oar barely stirred the reeds as he drifted under the bridge carrying his last quartet of tourists.

But it was more than a boat, and more than a night, and more than three-score years. And more than this earth, this sky even, and certainly more than any water that coursed through these streets or trembled from the sky.

They crossed, oh yes they crossed. And he is no longer Eliot, but his grandfather Clyde, looking for his Desdemona in the rain…

They'd clattered up the East Coast road by donkey-cart; black man, potagee woman; and Clyde would re-count in the years to come how the country women had come out of their doors in their saris, faces half-hidden, their menfolk at work in the fields. And stared. And how Clyde would do anything, no matter how hard times got, rather than join their husbands cane-cutting. The past is passed, he would grunt. Fieldwork would never, as long as he lived, shackle him to this red and bloody land.

And so they had settled amongst temples and mosques, in the shadow of cane-fields, which sprinkled their ash like black confetti. Desdemona's fair skin would leather under the sun, but her deep-water eyes locked in the story of a woman who had walked out of the sea and formed feet to walk on the earth. There she had been, waiting by the railway track at Kitty, coming from the seawall that long-ago morning. She had looked startled and when he looked into her eyes it was himself he had seen, drowning.

It was only by intimation that Clyde would tell Eliot about the passion, coughing loudly how his Desdemona nice nice eh? But he was old then, and rambling.

Eliot was old now too, had sold his bungalow after Joycelyn died and moved into the city itself. He'd joined the Historical Society and this was keeping him occupied now, after all the extra upset with his daughter, the daughter he'd never recognised, never knew.

History inhabited Eliot's mind daily, with each step he

took, Guyana and England swum through his mind like a pair of twin fish. He had told me part of his story, about Mother and Pa, Desiree, Joycelyn. But he hadn't told me about Clyde, or Desdemona, his maternal grandparents. Not that he knew much anyway, it was all fanciful really, and helped him to walk his walk between two worlds.

Looking round him now, in wet city streets, Eliot shook his head forcefully. He began to turn towards the car park behind the Marlowe Theatre when a soft voice, almost at his elbow, made him jump.

'*Big Issue,* Sir?'

Her pale face was surrounded by the hood of a red raincoat, and she looked stupidly, absurdly young. Her voice, when she spoke again, was as thin as the rain.

'*Big Issue,* Sir?'

He looked down at the damp pages of the magazines curling over the carrier bag she held close to her. On the whole he wasn't one for this sort of thing, and couldn't understand why these people just didn't get themselves a proper job, but all of a sudden she stumbled, and he automatically reached out an arm to steady her.

'Careful there, you all right?'

She was as light as the raincoat and before he knew it, her body slid through the offered arm and she fell sideways onto the wet street, carrier bags and magazines following.

'Good Lord! Hey Miss…!' He looked around wildly. There was no-one about. He dropped his briefcase and bent over her, shaking her small frame. 'Miss… Miss…!'

Her eyes fluttered open, startled, then looked frightened as they lit on him. She struggled to get up, waving away his offered arm. 'I'm okay. I'm okay…'

'You don't sound okay!' he looked around him again. The pub across the road had lights on, and he could see one or two heads against the leaded light windows.

'Come, let me buy you a drink.'

Heaven knows what he thought he was doing; he suspected what she needed was a good square meal, not that he was going to run to that but he was still a Christian wasn't he? Wasn't he?

She didn't argue, and stood rubbing her face with her wet hands as he picked up her carrier bag and followed him across the narrow street into the pub.

They walked into warm air, with the smell of hops, a fire and a quiet hum from the bar. He found himself thinking he should have asked her what she wanted; he didn't know what these young people drank nowadays, was it that alcopop stuff or beer from the bottle? But then this wasn't a social affair was it? It was medicinal, just the sort of thing for a shock. Sugar water was what he would have been given, what Desdemona stirred up for him when he was this girl's age, whatever her age was: she seemed no more than fifteen, but what did he know? They all looked like children to him, children running wild; children dressed half-naked in the cold, all their bellies and backsides hanging out and tattoos and the mouth on them, the mouth! Jesus, the obscenities he had borne witness to over the years! The loitering, the disrespect! One good slap, one good slap, that's all some of them needed, in Eliot's time any grown-up person could chastise you and no police would come and arrest you, and your parents would thank them because bad behaviour only brought disrespect. But then the whole world was different, wasn't it, and there was such a thing as society, even back in that under-developed country. Madness, madness.

'There's a table over there,' her small voice reached into his silent ravings. He'd almost forgotten her. Man, like he was getting to be a mad man in his old age.

She was shivering, and they moved towards the fireplace, to a narrow table built on sewing machine legs. Eliot read the *Singer* on the base, and remembered his mother sewing away in the gallery, making shirts for him and his father, at least until the day he got the scholarship and only a ready-made shirt from the Georgetown-based Kent Shirt Factory would do.

What did you talk to young people about anyway? It had been a long time since he'd been one, and he doubted whether his kind existed anymore, the kind that for whom riding a bicycle and smoking your first cigarette had been the heights.

Not for the first time Eliot felt himself a special kind of victim. Immigrant was a big word in this country. You had to be deaf and blind not to know about West Indian migration, about the mother country wanting bus drivers, about No Irish, No Dogs, No Blacks, about the New Cross fire, the Brixton riots, Handsworth. But not all emigrants were Windrush. The world had turned a billion times since that kind of migration, a whole world of lost souls, on a tsunami of dictators ranging from Amin to Saddam Hussein. And Eliot was another kind of immigrant, the type that blended in, had no issues of race or poverty or religion, only the fact that they were born a thousand miles away in a satellite of the mother country.

And this little waif he had picked up, what was her story? He saw them selling their *Big Issues* outside Tesco's, at the entrance to the underpass. He could understand the Eastern Europeans having that kind of trouble, but the English youngsters? With all the welfare and dole and housing benefit and tax credits? There was no such thing in his childhood, no such thing. The only homeless people then were beggars or madmen, and for the latter there was always the Berbice Mad House. Eliot had watched a programme on homelessness once and couldn't make head nor tail of it. People shouting, people sitting under Waterloo Station with wet dogs and pan-pipes, official-looking people saying that child abuse and unemployment caused it all. When all was said and done, the truth was that people just didn't look after their children because they were too busy looking after themselves, and the children all wanted to do things their own way, end of. So for the life of me he didn't know why he had to go and pick one of them up when he was happily thinking of his grand-parent's love story.

He looked around the pub, years since he'd been in a pub, well before the smoking ban. He may have given up himself a long time ago, but the place still seemed to lack atmosphere. Through the leaded windows the towers of the cathedral loomed up like the Marie Celeste.

What to do now? Go back to his little terrace house behind the newly re-named university, make his little dinner of smoked haddock and new potatoes with a touch of curry powder…

'Young lady…'

She looked squarely at him from under her scrap of hair.

He cleared his throat.

'Now I don't want you to get any funny ideas, and I am an old man now with no energy for any foolishness, but if you need somewhere to sleep until you sort yourself out, I have a spare room.'

He could read all the confusion in her eyes, see all the questions dancing there in the shadows. But somewhere deep inside, beneath all the madness he had come to sum up as life, something simple and clear like a torch was shining. Not everyone was given a second chance. Somewhere he knew she had a story to tell. While she was thinking about it, she might like to hear a few snippets of his.

'You know, in the country where I was born, if a child

fell down or anybody had any kind of shock, was sugar water they gave them, true-true.'

She lifted her head.

'What's sugar water?'

The Company of Women

If the land had a voice would it sing? Would it curse, would it condemn, would it praise? Would it allow itself to be owned, would it be a woman?

1989: halfway up the hill at Wye, Jessie was contemplating those questions. She was feeling anxious, worrying whether she had been wise to come. She had never had the bottle to do Snowdonia, or Anglesea, where these women went annually, doing brave things like climbing mountains and building rafts, but she could do Wye to Chilham surely? She was wearing her new Doc Martens, and a bright coloured skirt over leggings. She noticed some of the other women were wearing proper walking boots.

Eddie was away golfing that weekend, and her sister Rhona had come round for coffee earlier. Rhona had laughed at her.

'Weirdo! What do you look like?!'

She'd put her head back and looked her up and down in that stuck-up way she had.

'Oh, I dunno, first it's lesbians, now it's Art College. And Christ, those boots are so ugly. How on earth does Eddie put up with you?'

Jessie had ignored her, concentrated on packing her sandwiches into the new rucksack.

'Ta ra,' she'd said as she went out the door.

But on the way to the station her heart was hammering away inside her. She was one of only two heterosexual women going on the walk.

Not that it mattered, it wasn't supposed to matter.

She recalled the first time she'd gone along to a get-together, in Marie's house by the park.

'We welcome all women here,' Marie had said, guiding her through the house with narrow corridors through to the back with a hum of chit-chat and the aroma of sweetened tobacco. The faces turned towards her were welcoming, apart from two women from Canterbury with hardened faces and hair chopped off, with razors, or so it looked.

Jessie placed her wine offering down on a table laden with crisps and nuts, French bread, cheese, cans of beer. She was introduced to first one woman and then another, faces that turned in her direction, some open, some guarded. The conversation took off where it had lulled. They were talking about Greenham. In the background Tracy Chapman was singing.

Jessie found herself a seat on a floor cushion against the wall.

'We have to have an idea of numbers by Saturday,' someone said. 'We need to know if to go the whole hog with the coach or just the minibus.'

'Fifteen of the Canterbury women are coming, so that lets out the minibus.'

'That's still only half … let's do a head count…'

'Can I get you a top-up?', Jill asked.

Jessie nodded her thanks and passed her glass over. It had a ring of lipstick on it. She looked round, no-one else was wearing lipstick.

'Do you fancy going?' Jill said.

'Me?' Jessie laughed nervously. All she knew about Greenham was what she saw on the TV, angry protesters tying themselves to the railings and shaking their fists at the camera.

'Judy and Claire might come,' someone said. 'They couldn't make it tonight because of what's been going on, you know.'

'Oh, right! Well that's another two. How about you, Jill?'

'Oh I dunno if I can get anyone to look after the boys…'

'Won't your mum do it?'

'Only if I don't tell her where I'm going! You know what she's like!'

'Why not take them? There's loads of women and kids there; how else can we get them to learn about protecting the planet?'

'Oh, I'll have to let you know…'

Jessie sat back against the wall hoping no-one would ask her again.

They approached a wooded area and some of the group were way ahead.

'You can tell the toughies!' Jill caught her up, huffing and puffing. She was a good size 16, was Jill.

'Have you been walking with the group before?'

'A couple of times, but it was on the flat! Round the marshes, back in the spring, and a coastal walk by Dungeness, went to see Derek Jarman's garden. How about you, have you done much walking?'

'Oh no, not me! Not in this country…'

'You're from Zimbabwe aren't you? What brought you here?'

'Oh you know, my parents had to leave…'

Jessie was tired of explaining her migration. In the case of Zimbabwe she was more than tired of having to defend herself. Not many people had sympathy for ex-pat white farmers, not when there was so much inequality going on in the world. Jessie couldn't bring herself to talk about walking in the veld, or working on the farm with her parents. It was a life that was no longer real. She'd been woken up in the middle of the night and transported to another life just like that. It had been hard enough having to finish school in a strange country, making new friends, trying to fit in. Getting married had just kind of followed on.

They crested the hill and paused to catch their breath. The land rolled down beneath them, a patchwork weave of coppiced woodland, knitted hedgerows, splashes of vivid yellow, stippled fields pitted by sheep. On the hill opposite, the image of a crown was carved into the chalk. In a dip, the spire of Canterbury Cathedral.

'Wow!'

So this is England.

Jessie had lived the past eight years in East Kent and had never walked it. Drove it yes, biked it, bussed it, trained it. But walk, no way. She'd become a townie, had Jess, the job she'd just given up had been at the District Council 9 to 5; clubbing on Fridays, Asda's on Saturdays. Her girlfriends had been more wine bar than country stiles. Hubby clean, reasonably considerate. She wondered how much art college would change all that. She'd already got the DMs. (Which were pinching a bit.)

'I wasn't expecting this!'

'Yeah, that's pretty amazing!'

The others were waiting ahead.

'Women, are you out for a Sunday stroll, or a bloody good walk?' Judith, the serious one, looked up from staring at the map weatherproofed in its plastic sleeve, strung round her neck.

'I think we hug the hedge as far as this field then cross diagonally over there…'

They clambered over the stile, and headed along a rough path framed on one side by overgrown brambles and blackthorn. Jessie wondered why she'd bothered to wear a skirt over her leggings, it caught on the brambles, and was making her sweat. Jill had gone on ahead and was walking with Marie. Jessie found herself bringing up the rear. It brought back a sick lonely feeling, like she used to have in school. Girls: giggling and walking together, in pairs along corridors or on school trips. Not like Jessie, new, with a funny accent. Don't be silly, she told herself, we're just walking, each at our own pace, and these women *like* you, they do.

They reached the field that Judith had indicated, but there was some debate. Some thought they should carry on until the next. Jessie stood and waited. There was a sweet smell in the air, it hung over them like a pungent cloud. She wrinkled her nose.

'It's the rape,' Marie said, 'Did you see it from up top? They're planting a lot of it now. Not much good for my hay-fever.'

They followed Judith across the field, but then came to a complete dead-end.

'I told you this was wrong,' said Debs. She was Judith's partner.

'It's not fucking wrong!' Judith exclaimed, 'Look, we've followed the right path, it's the bastard farmer who's blocked it, look! New wire fencing all along here! Gob-shite!'

'Oh it's a man then is it?' Debs laughed.

'Bound to be! What woman in her right mind would block a foot-path? These paths have been right of way for hundreds of bloody years! Who'd change the law of the land to suit himself but a bloody fat fascist farmer!?'

'Why don't we just have a sit and a drink?' Marie offered. 'Look! It's so beautiful! And peaceful! You'd never guess trains and roads were anywhere nearby.'

They spread jumpers and jackets down on the meadow grass, rummaged in rucksacks for bottles of water and cordial, shared segments of orange, breathed in the air. Bees hummed.

'Hey look … what's that?'

There was a movement ahead in the long grass, agitated chirping, a flash of wings upwards.

'Oh it's a skylark, trying to distract us, bless him! Obviously got a nest nearby, do you think?'

It was on the tip of Jessie's lips to mention some of the names and birdsong she had grown up hearing – from the rhythmic repetition of the cisticola birds – the winding cisticola, the chirping cisticola, the tinkling cisticola – to the stripe-cheeked bulbul, the African swift…

The voices of the women rose and fell like the skylark, immersed in his antics, dipping after them even as they rose and retraced their steps.

Marie joined her as they skirted the field, finding another way back to the track.

'Feel like a proper pilgrim I do; they reckon this is the route they took. Can you imagine it, plodding over hill and dale, just to go and pray?' She paused; then added, 'Did I tell you Ava's moving in with me?'

'No way! Thought you guys were against all that domestic stuff!'

Marie shrugged. 'Oh well, we have a reason now…'

'Yeah…?'

'Well, I'm kind of like … pregnant…'

'What?' Jessie stopped in her tracks. 'So did all that fuss with the syringe work?'

Marie blushed. 'No. We actually went through a clinic.'

'Oh.' Jessie didn't know what to say. She was confused about how she felt about some things. She could see her father, thin-lipped and serious, her mother, apron on, giving instructions to the black gardener.

Eddie now; she couldn't compare him to her stolid father but how many times had she gone along to the women's group feeling like shit and just sat quietly, soaking up the atmosphere and listening to the women engage in political debate? And how many times had they commented on her silence, and tried to draw her out on how she felt? It wasn't as if Eddie stopped her doing anything, or beat her up, or emotionally abused her. It was just a series of small things … the way he laughed if she expressed an opinion that was different from his, the way he introduced her at his works do, *Here's the little missus*; the strong feelings he had against homosexuality, the way he expected life to follow the pattern he had set. 'I'll live and die here,' he would say, eye on his garden, if she ever indicated her restlessness. And after sex, watching him fall asleep instantly, how could she describe that slightly … disappointed feeling?

Jessie didn't know either why she felt heady when she was in the company of these women, whether it was the smell of them, fresh shampoo, or herb soap, even Jill with her hippie patchouli oil, or whether it was the raw energy that existed when they were all together, their emotional truisms, their articulacy, their knowledge and enquiry that nudged her awareness awake, opened doors for her. She doubted whether she'd be embarking on her course now, if it hadn't been for them.

There was a commotion up ahead, loud shrieks and

flapping arms. She and Marie speeded up to find Judith on her back in a gap in the hedge, trying to disentangle herself from brambles. Her map had broken its string and lay face up in a nearby cowpat. Debs was bent over laughing, her hands on her knees, whilst Judith glowered up at her. Her laughter was contagious and spread amongst them, punctuated by banter and Debs' laughter turning to hiccups. Jessie felt a small bubble lifting from the tightness in her chest.

As the walk got underway again, Jessie thought about that laughter, which had completely extinguished her self-consciousness. The one constant, she realised, in all those house parties with these women, was laughter, laughter in the face of adversity, laughter on the point of pain, laughter at the silliest things. As she walked down the old trackway, the history of which Marie was explaining, Jessie felt like she was a seedling newly pushed into the earth, needing to nestle further into rough darkness, needing to turn her face to the wall of earth, which she knew would mother her, hold her close in its embrace until she was ready to face the light without blinking.

Her hands felt heavy at her side. She raised them and noticed her fingers were swollen.

'Oh Lord.'

'What is it?' Marie paused, and looked down at Jessie's fingers. 'Don't worry, that's normal. Lift your arms up a bit as you walk, that'll keep the blood flowing.'

They'd reached the field of rape.

'Christ, that's tall! I didn't realise it grew so tall!'

Jill came up behind them. 'Do we have to walk through that? Just as well I took my tabs before coming!'

'Why do they call it call it rape?'

Marie shrugged. 'Dunno. Bit harsh, especially since it's quite pretty really.'

The smell was strong and heady. Jessie took a deep

breath. Zimbabwe seemed to float away as if in a dream. The field in front of her stretched away golden and scented. The sun, grudging so far, begun to spread its warmth right into her bones. The path was overgrown but as she approached, the plants appeared to part for her. Her boots were no longer pinching, they seemed to have moulded themselves around her feet; seemed to know where they were going. And the land, this land on which she had barely skimmed across, like a virginal dragonfly, begun to make itself known to her, through the soles of her feet.

Ferry me softly

1978

What is it about water that people always have to stop and stare? They got off at Canterbury West station and walked up through the Westgate Towers. The babies were screaming from being cooped up in the pushchairs and so they headed straight up the High Street for Ricemans Department Stores. The High Street was packed as usual, ahead of them the crowd swayed as if in a desert haze. By the time they got to the Weavers Bridge they were ramming the pushchairs into French legs and Swedish knees, as everyone stopped to look down at the water. It wasn't even as if there was much of it. What there was, was weedy, there was no wildlife to speak of, no crocs or flamingos. But they'd always stop and have a look anyway.

The boatman was ferrying a group of students whose

heads disappeared under the bridge.

'We'll have to treat ourselves one of these days,' Joss said.

Marli laughed and flicked back her long brown hair. 'With what? You seen the prices? It's either that or dinner!'

'How much you got to spend then?'

'Ten quid.'

'He was feeling generous then?'

'Better than last time! That's the problem when you have to depend on someone else for money.'

'You still thinking of that part-time job?'

Marli shrugged as they walked on. Dominic was still screaming. She rubbed his head briefly.

'Be there in a minute baby, Mummy change you.'

They headed quickly past the shop windows where alluring models posed in maxi-dresses and wedge-heeled shoes. They'd have a look later. Gone were the days when they could just saunter in and out of shops. Ricemans was the only store with a decent toilet to change the babies but that was three floors up. They waited for the lift and then juddered up to the third floor, where a well-dressed old lady wearing white gloves beamed down at the babies.

'You two girls have got your hands full,' she said.

They took turns to use the loo, each jostling a wriggling child on their laps as they changed diapers.

'At least I'm glad I'm not breast-feeding anymore,' Joss said, lips holding a nappy pin. 'You know, when me and Ted were in the States last year we went to this mall and you should have seen the facilities – special Mother and Baby rooms! And throw-away nappies too, would you believe it!'

'Really? That would make things easier wouldn't it? This country's bloody rubbish, don't know why my mum had to emigrate here instead of a decent country like Canada.'

'She still working at the hospital?'

'Yep, wiping bums, washing floors.'

Joss sighed. 'Um, sad innit, from what you said.'

They waited by the lift.

'Might as well look at the kids' clothes aye? We were thinking of getting Carly christened.'

'Are you? That'll be lovely! But it's a bit expensive here.'

'Oh, let's have a look anyway.'

They wheeled the buggies through the menswear department to the children's section. Joss headed for the baby rail, sliding hangers and pulling out christening gowns one after the other. Marli watched her eyes grow big at the prices.

'She's a bit big for all these now,' she sighed. 'Should have done it months ago.'

'Why didn't you?'

'Oh, Ted ain't really into church stuff; sez they're all perverts and mind twisters, but the way I see it, it's blessing a child innit and you got to believe in something.'

'Well you can always just get her a nice white dress; summer stuff's in the shops already, you're bound to find something. How old is Carly now … eight months?'

Joss nodded, 'Yes, on Friday.'

'Well you might be better off looking in Temple's in Ramsgate; they got some lovely children's clothes in there. That's where I got Dominic his dungarees.'

'Yeah,' Joss said slowly, still fondling the lace collar on a gown.

'Come on,' Marli said firmly, 'it's not all about the kids anyway. Let's go find something for us; I need to get something for Saturday. You *are* going to Felicity's barbecue aren't you?'

They took the lift down again and wandered through Marks and Sparks which was just full of old people's stuff. Then Dorothy Perkins, Chelsea Girl and C&As where

Marli tried on a blue maxi-dress with a halter-neck tie.

'Buy it,' Joss said assertively, 'looks good on you. How much is it?'

'£5.99…'

'There you go; you got enough to buy me lunch now!'

They turned down one of the side streets leading to the Cathedral, where a throng of loud French students were being rounded up and guided through the archway.

'Poor things,' Joss said, 'I bet they'd much rather go to Margate.'

1983

'I feel I'm missing something,' said Joss. They'd just got off the train and were walking up Canterbury High Street.

Marli stopped to put Mimi's dummy back in her mouth.

'Your brain maybe?' she said smiling.

'Yeah, that and all. A bloody pushchair, that's what. I still can't get used to them both being at school now. I don't know what to do with my hands!'

'Is that why you've taken up smoking? You must have had three on the train!'

'Don't you nag me and all! It's stressful, working now and coming home still expected to do stuff.'

Marli paused outside Barnados.

'You're not going in *there* are you?' Joss said.

'You can get some good stuff in there, especially kids clothes. They're not in them five minutes are they?'

'Well hurry up, you know we've got to get back for the other kids.'

The usual crowd of tourists were leaning over the Weavers Bridge. Marli and Joss stopped and looked over. The water was low, and the boatman stood on the wooden stage looking bored. 'Why don't we have a ride?' Joss suggested, 'I got my wages, could treat us…?'

Marli made a face. 'Naw, thanks anyway, but can you imagine trying to keep Mimi still? She's such a fidget! Trust me to have another precocious child! I 'd better pop into Mothercare and change her.'

'So how's things?' Joss asked.

Marli shrugged. 'Mean as ever, I'm working nights now at Hornby's.'

'Is he still going out every week?'

'Yep. Stayed in for a few weeks after I had Mimi but then back to his old ways.'

'Oh, maybe it's just a boy thing. Ted played pool with him a couple of weeks ago.'

'Far as I know, they close the club at 11. He came in at 1 o'clock in the morning last Friday.'

'Really?' Joss stopped and put a quick arm round Marli's shoulder. 'Have you had it out with him?'

Marli rustled in her bag for a tissue and blew her nose. 'Oh yeah. Stayed up and confronted him. Talked, cried, smashed his beer mug. *'Spect me to sit in 'ere night after night wiv you?* he said. Drunk as a skunk.'

'Christ.'

'Never mind me,' Marli said, 'How're you and Ted?'

'We're plodding on; he got promoted last month so when he comes home he has his dinner and just crashes out. I'm doing more with working now that I ever did, having to fit in everything.'

'We should have a night out.'

'Yes, why don't we?'

They crossed into St Margaret's Street and went into Mothercare. Joss looked round approvingly in the new baby changing room.

'I heard they'd done this up … wish they'd had all this when mine were babies! Remember balancing them on our laps?!'

'Yes, don't I! But you still don't see no dads in here do

you?' She folded the disposable nappy in a tidy packet and tossed it in the bin.

'Might as well have a look round while we're here,' Marli said as they walked back through the floor. 'They've got their summer things in already … look at these titchy little Hawaiian shirts…!'

It was market day in Canterbury, though most of the traders did Ramsgate as well. No point in buying stuff in Canterbury you could get in Ramsgate. They rifled through the new season's clothes in Benetton – Africa was *in* this year, lots of khaki shorts and 'ethnic' prints.

'Don't know why I'm bothering looking,' Marli said grumpily. 'I'm getting that fat. Imagine me in this, I'd look a right cow.'

'You've got the udders to go with it!' quipped Joss, just dodging Marli's cuff. 'At least you've got your own money now,' she added, laughing.

'Yeah, but I'm expected to get all the food for three kids and us out of it. Me working has just meant he has more money to spend in the pub.'

'Me working at Littlewoods isn't any great shakes. And a man asleep is better than one on the street.'

They decided on Debenhams for lunch. The entrance to the restaurant was directly opposite the Cathedral, and a burst of laughter came from a group of young punks outside The Olive Branch pub. They all sported Mohican haircuts, in dazzling shades of pink, orange and green.

The girls looked at each other.

'Do you ever get the feeling time's moving on and leaving you behind?'

They sighed and shared carrying Mimi's pushchair downstairs to the restaurant. They had a hot lunch, lasagne and salad, talked about taking up yoga at the Adult Education, and where their kids were at in school.

By the time they'd eaten it was almost two, time to head back to the station. The Benetton bag slapped against the handle of the pushchair.

1995

'Marli!'

Marli turned her head at the sound of her name.

A tubby spiky-haired young woman in Doc Martens was coming out of the British Heart Foundation shop.

'Joss?'

The two women stood back and looked at each others' faces, then embraced.

'My God look at you!'

'Look at *you!*' Joss reached out and touched Marli's blonde highlights.

'You've not been in *there* have you?! Thought you didn't do charity shops?'

'Why give the fascists your hard-earned money?'

They went for a drink in Alberry's wine bar.

'…well the kids were all doing their own thing you know, and I decided it was time for me. Littlewoods was planning to close down, and I thought long and hard about what to do next. Did I want to be a shop-girl all my life? So I did an Access Course at Thanet College and now I'm doing Sociology at Christ Church here in Canterbury.'

Marli raised her glass. 'Well done you! But what the hell use is an ology? You're better off doing hairdressing aintcha? Christ, it must be three or four years since I've seen you! '

'Well, what about you? What are you up to?' Joss sat back and looked at her friend. How had they let time interrupt their friendship? She thought of their days out to Canterbury whilst the kids were young, and some of the house parties with mutual friends.

'Hey do you remember that night we decided to go clubbing in Margate?' she laughed.

'Do I just! Me and you like two old dogs in maxi-dresses! No-one told us they'd gone out of fashion!'

'That's what having kids does for you!'

Marli took a swallow of her wine. 'Me and the pig split up in the end.'

Joss knew this but didn't say.

'...found out he was having it off with some slapper from Newington. So I took the initiative, changed the locks, chucked his stuff into black bin bags and left them outside the bitch's door.'

'Woah!'

'Course the kids were gutted, thought the sun shone out his bleeding arse.' She looked straight at Joss. 'I couldn't tell you half the shit. And workwise ... well, at least I got out of the factory.'

'So you're not there anymore?'

'No. I'm crap, who'd employ me?'

They walked back down the High Street. Passed the Weavers. Looked over the bridge. Nothing.

'Must have packed up early,' Joss said. 'Look, let's not leave it so long next time eh?'

2011

Marli got off the Park and Ride bus by Fenwicks. She stood on the pavement, trying to get her bearings. She still found it alienating when she came to Canterbury. So much had changed. Look at the bus station now, all glass and posh seats, new information centre, the blokes directing the buses in like aircraft groundsmen. She caught sight of herself in Fenwicks' window. Old, she looked old. She patted her hair, short now. She wandered through the precinct, glitzy with all these shops. She could barely remember what had been there before. Hadn't this been the back entrance of Ricemans? The shop-girls there had been well snooty. She remembered just peering in at the hairdressers on the top-floor once. And didn't you use to be able to walk from there through to Marks? Well it was all gone now. Though she quite liked the new Marks, or maybe she'd grown into it. Like Bonmarché. She laughed to herself, and looked up and down the street. Woolworths had gone too. And the nice old post office building was a Mexican and you had to go upstairs in Smiths and queue for half hour for a bleed-ing stamp. Her footsteps led her down the High Street. It was the first time she'd come through the city from this direction; normally she'd have come by train, and walked through from Canterbury West. She smiled to herself as she thought of her little Fiat.

She stood by the Weavers and waited for Joss. In her hand she clutched some leaflets from the Tourist Informa-tion Centre: The Canterbury Tales Attraction, Canterbury Museum, Canterbury Cathedral.

'Hey girl!' Joss appeared by her side suddenly. She looked thin. Not good thin, sickly thin. But Marli smiled and kissed her on the cheek.

'Hi Joss, good to see you! Did you come in on the train?'

She nodded.'Yeah, I'm not as clever as you. What have you got there?'

Marli held out the leaflets. 'Well you know we've been promising ourselves this trip for how many years? So, I thought, now that we've got time on our hands, maybe we should do it all!'

'All?' Joss frowned. 'Take more than a day to do it all properly.'

'Yes I know that, we'll just have to keep having days out won't we? Just think all the years we've been coming to Canterbury we never did anything *cultural*. Too busy wandering in and out of shops buying rubbish! I tell you,

I've got more clothes and shoes than that Marcos woman! Besides, who's going to look at me now?'

'Don't do yourself down, Marli, look how you've sorted your life out over the past few years…'

'Yes, I know…'

'The only thing an ology did was give me this flipping cancer,' Joss said bitterly.

Marli didn't know what to say; she didn't want to say it was the fags.

'Come on,' she said, brightly, 'let's go, we've waited long enough.'

The boatman helped them into the boat.

'Hello ladies, welcome aboard.' He waited for them to settle. It was early in the season so they were the only ones.

They grasped the side of the boat as he gently pushed off from the small jetty with the oar.

'So, where are you two ladies from?' he asked.

The burst of laughter was muted as the boat glided under the bridge.

Epilogue

Well, I never promised you one.

Cultured Llama Publishing

hungry for poetry
thirsty for fiction

Cultured Llama was born in a converted stable. This creature of humble birth drank greedily from the creative source of the poets, writers, artists and musicians that visited, and soon the llama fulfilled the destiny of its given name.

Cultured Llama is a publishing house, a multi-arts events promoter and a fundraiser for charity. It aspires to quality from the first creative thought through to the finished product.

www.culturedllama.co.uk

Also published by Cultured Llama

A Radiance
by Bethany W. Pope

Paperback; 70pp; 203 x 127 mm;
978-0-9568921-3-3; June 2012
Cultured Llama

Family stories and extraordinary images glow throughout this compelling debut collection from an award-winning author, like the disc of uranium buried in her grandfather's backyard. *A Radiance* 'gives glimpses into a world both contemporary and deeply attuned to history – the embattled history of a family, but also of the American South where the author grew up.'

> 'A stunning debut collection... these poems invite us to reinvent loss as a new kind of dwelling, where the infinitesimal becomes as luminous as ever.'
>
> Menna Elfyn

'*A Radiance* weaves the voices of four generations into a rich story of family betrayal and survival, shame and grace, the visceral and sublime. A sense of offbeat wonder at everyday miracles of survival and love both fires these poems and haunts them – in a good way.'

Tiffany S. Atkinson

'An exhilarating and exceptional new voice in poetry.'

Matthew Francis

Also published by Cultured Llama

strange fruits
by Maria C. McCarthy

Paperback; 72pp; 203 x 127 mm;
978-0-9568921-0-2; July 2011
Cultured Llama (in association with
WordAid.org.uk)

Maria is a poet of remarkable skill, whose work offers surprising glimpses into our 21st-century lives – the 'strange fruits' of our civilisation or lack of it. Shot through with meditations on the past and her heritage as 'an Irish girl, an English woman', *strange fruits* includes poems reflecting on her urban life in a Medway town and as a rural resident in Swale.

Maria writes, and occasionally teaches creative writing, in a shed at the end of her garden.

All profits from the sale of *strange fruits* go to Macmillan Cancer Support, Registered Charity Number 261017.

'Maria McCarthy writes of the poetry process: "There is a quickening early in the day" ('Raising Poems'). A quickening is certainly apparent in these humane poems, which are both natural and skilful, and combine the earthiness and mysterious-ness of life. I read *strange fruits* with pleasure, surprise and a sense of recognition.' Moniza Alvi, author of *Europa*